CW00594581

BETTER OFF UNDEAD

BETTER OFF UNDEAD

PROVIDENCE PARANORMAL COLLEGE BOOK SEVEN

D.R. PERRY

DISRUPTIVE IMAGINATION

This book is a work of fiction. All of the characters, organizations, and events portrayed in this novel are either products of the author's imagination or are used fictitiously. Sometimes both.

Copyright © 2016 D.R. Perry
Cover by Fantasy Book Design
Cover copyright © LMBPN Publishing

LMBPN Publishing supports the right to free expression and the value of copyright. The purpose of copyright is to encourage writers and artists to produce the creative works that enrich our culture.

The distribution of this book without permission is a theft of the author's intellectual property. If you would like permission to use material from the book (other than for review purposes), please contact support@lmbpn.com. Thank you for your support of the author's rights.

LMBPN Publishing
PMB 196, 2540 South Maryland Pkwy
Las Vegas, NV 89109

Version 2.0 June, 2021
ebook ISBN: 978-1-64971-841-9
Print ISBN: 978-1-64971-842-6

CHAPTER ONE

Speed Dumping

"It's not you, it's me." Della Dawn sighed, her voice more dramatic than the entire Rhode Island College Theatre Department. I knew, because they'd performed in Night Creatures' last indie-produced music video, along with Della, of course.

"Seriously?" I blinked, then stared at my soon to be ex-girlfriend's static expression, marveling at the fact that her voice could be this expressive with her face still as a stone. I'd always found that trait of hers one of the most interesting things about her. Well, besides the fact that she smelled amazing. All the other vampires I knew thought so, too. Except for my guitarist, Matt.

"I think we should see other people, Lane." Della's hands curled around the hot coffee I'd just brought her.

"Well, I don't." I wished I had a cup to hide my anguish instead of empty hands that trembled until I pressed them flat on the table. But of course, vampires don't drink coffee, so I'd saved my money like an idiot.

"You could have fooled me." Della's left shoulder lifted, displaying a lacy bra strap under her off-the-shoulder blouse. I

1

couldn't help but stare at the shoulder she'd probably never let me touch again.

"What do you mean?"

"I mean, you play at that Nocturnal Lounge for free all year, play a party for that dude-bro Redcap, and vanish to who knows where that whole night and the next without me." Della didn't pout. Maybe if she had that whole train-wreck of a month might have gone down differently. "You only think about your band, Lane, and they're not even that big a deal. Some girls might be able to deal with that, but I'm not one of them."

I blinked again and took a deep breath through my nose, which only made the whole thing worse. All I smelled was her perfume and the way it perfectly enhanced the scent of her blood. Being a vampire already sucked, but getting dumped made it even worse. By the time I opened my mouth to try to convince Della to stay, it was too late.

The sway of her hips was brisk and deliberate as she turned her back on me and walked out of Blue State Coffee. I stared, only managing to get my eyes above waist level to notice her holding that nearly fresh cup of coffee by the lid, with one hand. She held it over the trash can, let it dangle for half a second, then dropped it in. Della pushed the glass instead of the handle to open the door, leaving her fingerprints all over it just like everything else she'd touched. Then, she stepped across the threshold under the red-lit exit sign.

And I couldn't move. I felt as trashed as that coffee she'd tossed, the potential of actually having a decent evening leaking out like her discarded brew out of the paper cup. The only impulse I had just then was to cover my face with both hands and sob. But I refused to be that stereotypical vampire guy, ugly-crying in the middle of a busy coffee shop right before a poetry slam. I got up and let my feet take me away because they had to know more about where to go from here than my blindsided heart and mind.

Out on the street, I hunched my shoulders, my hands in my pockets. Yeah, I guess I had something to hide. Maybe I should have told Della more of what was going on with me after Fred's farewell party. I got chased around Providence by a creepy dude in a yellow suit, ending up in the freaking Under of all places because an imp and a crazy cat shifter played me harder than Eddie Van Halen usually whaled on his guitar.

What had stopped me? There'd always been something special about Della Dawn. She had this effect on me, the kind that ties stomachs up in knots and infests them with butterflies. We'd been serious for three months, from the night I noticed her leaning against the back wall of The Living Room at a gig, right up to that slow walk she'd taken out of Blue State Coffee. That was a long time for me to date someone. Even before I got turned, I hadn't done much more than date a girl for a few weeks or have "special friend fun time" with groupies and barflies. I'd really thought Della and I were going somewhere, that we might even be destined like my friend Henry and his girl Maddie, but clearly, Della wasn't on that bandwagon.

I sighed, staring down at the Sharpie-decorated toes of my Converse All-Stars. That was why I ran headfirst into the staple-studded telephone pole and tore a few layers of skin off my forehead. I wondered whether it was in the shape of the letter L for "loser." Then I glanced around, hoping no one had snapped a pic on their phone and sent it to the vampire tip line. I didn't think Josh Dennison's mom would press charges against me for spacing out over a breakup.

It's against the law for vamps to walk around with an injury this obvious. So if I don't act fast I could end up spending most of the night in the clink. That would have been insult added to injury and just my luck lately. That night, my life seemed worse than the cynical movie character Mom had named me after.

"Yo, Lane." Pete clapped me on the shoulder, almost knocking me over in the process. What can I say? Drummers tend to have powerful arms, but Pete also had a Psychic power that enhanced his strength even more than most vampires'. He grinned, not daring to bare his fangs by smiling on a street as crowded as Thayer. "You gashed your head pretty bad. Get in the van."

I nodded, bowing my head and letting my buddy guide me to the battered old vehicle we usually piled into for gigs. In the back, Pete handed me a bag of blood from the cooler we always kept stocked. I drank it fast, applying the undead regenerative energy directly to my forehead.

"Why the long face, Mister Meyer?" The flat-voweled voice from the front seat belonged to Matt Gardner, Night Creatures' guitarist.

"Della dumped me." There wasn't any point in fibbing about something like that with Matt around. He had some kind of lie-detecting Psychic ability. Our absent bassist had Telekinesis, but a weak enough form that he only bothered with it to keep his glasses from falling off. I was the only member of the Night Creatures with nothing special in the powers department. Just the fangs and sunlight allergy for good old Lane, apparently.

"Lame." Pete shook his head. "But I think I've got just the remedy for your problem." He rummaged on the floor, then held up a flier in one massive hand. "It's Vampire Speed-Dating night over at Cafe Paragon."

Before I could protest, Pete pushed me out of the back of the van. I heard the driver's side door close, and the locks engage when Matt left the vehicle. He pocketed the keys, the gesture bouncing his dreads. My bandmates flanked me, walking along on either side so I couldn't just high-tail it for some other part of the city. I walked back up Thayer Street, staring straight ahead. When we got to the big red and silver sign on the corner, I took a deep breath I didn't physically need and went inside.

The speed-dating people had taken over half the place. Round tables had metal stands in the middle, cardboard cubes with numbers painted on the sides impaled on them like heads on spikes. I turned to walk back out the door, but a solid wall of Pete stopped me. I sighed and headed over to the lady scribbling names and contact information on a clipboard.

"Ohmigosh, you're not serious?" The blonde woman smiled brightly, as though wanting to show the world she wasn't a vampire. "We have half the Night Creatures here to speed-date too?"

"What do you mean, too?" I turned my head, squinting at her out of the corner of my right eye.

"Oh, it's not important." She beamed like the headlights on a four by four, or maybe an overpriced hatchback. "Just sign in, mmkay?" She pushed the clipboard at me in a distinctly unlady-like fashion. Just as I was starting to relax and appreciate the absurdity of this situation, I saw the reason why Miss Smiley had said, "too."

The Jack Steele Band was there, each member already seated at a numbered table. They always beat us in the qualifiers for Newport's Battle of The Bands, and we'd entered religiously since 1998, before we got turned. Also, I knew Jack from way back. He'd been my guitar teacher before the Reveal, and during part of it, even. Apparently, he'd been good enough at hiding his vampirism to avoid most of the mess that came when extrahumans got outed to the general public. After he'd registered as a vampire, he'd turned into one creepy dude. At first I thought it was an act, but there were rumors associating him with an illegal blood Doll ring ten years ago. Unfortunately, my predicament was even worse than just running into my old, shady teacher.

We'd arrived at Paragon for the second round of speed-dating. Jack and his eponymous band had gotten there first, so they already had ladies sitting across from them. And guess who occupied the other seat at Jack's table, giggling at the jerk while hanging on his every word?

Della Dawn, that's who.

"Shazbot." Matt was straightedge and didn't swear. Ever.

Claimed it helped him keep his urges under control or something. He dragged Pete out of my way, understanding that there was no way I'd stick around to watch that. To his credit, once Pete noticed the situation, he grumbled and came along with us.

My bandmates followed me out, something that pissed me off at first. But when I turned down Angell Street headed for Lovecraft Square, I changed my mind. Having Matt and Pete with me turned out to be a good thing. I turned left to take the long way down the Trolley Tunnel because its darkness matched my mood. After it was too late to turn around, I heard a gritty voice saying words no almost-famous vampire ever wanted to hear.

"Mr. Meyer, we'd like a moment of your time." A dude Pete's size grinned, stepping away from the patch of wall he'd been leaning on.

"Wouldn't everyone?" I shook my head. "This really isn't a good time."

"Mr. Gitano sends his regards." A second voice, still deep but more like a diving pool than the deep blue whatever, came from behind us.

"Tony can send me regards in person. It's not like he doesn't know where to find me." I shrugged and took a step toward the Nocturnal Lounge end of the tunnel.

"Um, Lane?" Matt poked me in the back with a finger. "Um, I don't think these guys mean Tony when they're talking about Mr. Gitano."

"And why is that, Matt?" I thought I might know, but hoped I was dead wrong.

"Um—" Matt mumbled something I couldn't have comprehended even if I'd been a Telepathic Psychic. His constant "um-ing" was getting on my last nerve, too. I snarled, turning my head to bare my fangs at him. I backed down when I saw how freaked out he was. But the Gatto Gang thugs interrupted.

"Because you owe something to Mr. Gitano, Mr. Meyer." The owner of the second voice peeled off from the wall, stepping closer to us than the other guy had. I could make out his face. I knew him, too.

"Paul Armati." I knew Paul was one of the newer enforcers in the Gatto Gang. And I knew Fred's aunt, who used to babysit him. I grinned, letting my mind make a bunch of goofy pictures for the appearance of bravado, but it didn't improve my mood. "Wish I could say it's good to see you, but like I said, this night's lousier than a fleabag motel. Bad news city. So, you guys have my phone number. Call any time that isn't tonight, okay?"

"We can't do that, Mr. Meyer."

"Dude, call me Lane, okay?" I sighed, realizing I couldn't exactly blow off organized crime guys, who also shape-shifted into large predators in a dark alley no matter how much I wanted to. "Mr. Meyer's my father." I didn't add that he only acted like a dad when the Alzheimer's let him remember that fact. But I wasn't about to auto-correct my slip-up and show weakness in front of these guys.

"Okay, Lane." Paul held his hands slightly out from his sides with the palms in, a posture I knew meant he was ready for trouble. "Well, like I said, you owe Mr. Gitano. And he's got an idea that'll help you clear your debt to him."

"Let's forget for a minute that I don't know what I owe him or how I came to owe it." I shot a dirty look over at Matt, who seemed to know more about this than his Psychic polygraph power should reveal. "What's this idea?"

"The Newport Battle of the Bands is coming up at the end of the month." Paul smiled. "And Mr. Gitano wants Night Creatures to win it."

I blinked, not understanding how that idea would work, anyway. It made absolutely no sense in so many ways I could barely get my brain around the concept. I opened my mouth, but Pete beat me to the punch. That was fine with me. I didn't like confrontation.

"But we didn't qualify for the Battle of the Bands last month." Pete scratched his head. "We can't win if we ain't qualified."

"Oh, but you did qualify." Paul's smile got even bigger, his bicuspids and canines slightly longer than before and his usually brown eyes going greenish with a vertical slit. If his animal side popped out like this when he was in a good mood, I definitely did not want to deal with the enforcer in a bad mood.

"And how did we manage that?" I tilted my head to the side briefly, then righted it. The last thing I wanted was to look like a moron. It was probably too late for that, though.

"Technicality." Paul practically purred. "The band slated to challenge the Jack Steele Band, well let's just say both their guitarists had unrelated and unfortunate hand accidents. And Night Creatures was next on the list."

"So, what do you think?" The other guy cracked his knuckles.

"Sounds like a great idea to me." I didn't even care anymore about the mysterious and probably shady debt. All I could think about now was finally being able to prove my band was better than my old music teacher's. And, of course, convince Della she'd made the wrong choice about dumping me for that old Jazz Era has-been. "We'll do it."

Paul chuckled, then turned his back on us. I listened to his footsteps, and his associate's as the pair of goons brushed by us toward the nearer tunnel exit. Matt breathed a sigh of relief way bigger than any self-respecting vampire should have been holding.

"See, John?" I heard Paul's commentary echo back at us. "Told you it was an offer he couldn't refuse."

"But how in the hell are we going to beat the Jack Steele Band, Lane?" Pete practically wailed the question the big green monster had pushed completely out of my head. We'd never beaten anyone in any of the music contests, never even won a local award. All we had going for us was popularity with non-industry people. It was entirely possible we'd all be at increased risk of unfortunate hand accidents or worse ourselves if Gitano thought we couldn't win.

"No idea, Pete." I smacked my forehead with the palm of one hand, curling the other into a fist. Then, I walked up the tunnel, toward the only place I might find a sympathetic ear, maybe even a little help, and knocked on the wall.

CHAPTER TWO

Lounge Lizard

I leaned my forehead against the concrete wall of the old Trolley Tunnel, fist rapping the knocking pattern that'd let daylight-averse students at Providence Paranormal College through the secret door. Of course, my feet had auto-piloted to the Nocturnal Lounge. I murmured a few choice words, thinking the door wouldn't open. It was summer vacation, after all. But I thought wrong. The concrete vanished, granting me access to the stairs.

No one would be there, I thought as I headed up. Even Lynn Frampton, the brainy human majoring in PPC's equivalent of extrahuman pre-med, had only enrolled in online courses for the summer sessions. But when I got through the door, I discovered I couldn't have been more wrong. I peered down from the mezzanine into what looked like an impending brawl.

"Can it, cat brains!" Blaine Harcourt actually stood, glaring down at a trench-coated fellow instead of just making his eyes roll from a sofa somewhere.

"Oh, go molt or something, scale-tail!" Tony turned his back on Blaine, stalking over to the coffee counter. Even though he was in human form, I imagined the cat shifter with a fluffy gray tail, tip flicking angrily behind him.

"You turn around and say that to my face, or I'll cook up some feline flambé right here and now!" Blaine growled, the cloud of smoke around his head thicker than I'd ever seen it. He looked like a one-man smoking section, except for the orange-tinted scales popping up along his arms. That was one more angry fire-dragon shifter than I wanted to be around. I almost turned and left.

"Cut it out, both of you." Kimiko Ichiro held up one hand, nose still nearly pressed against the tablet in her other hand. "Bianca's trying to concentrate on the reason we're here."

"But your boy-toy asked for it, Kim." Tony tossed his coffee stirrer into the trash. "He's a guest here, remember? The Nocturnal Lounge is my house, and I don't put up with Trogdor threatening to burninate the place or anyone in it."

"I don't care who started it." The petite brunette stood, finally setting her electronic device down to put her hands on her hips. "Tony, you have to chill out and stop poking the dragon. And you need to relax, Blaine. Because Bianca isn't going to find anything out if you scare all the ghosts off by going all *Dragonball-Z* in here. Look, I'm the last person to not want you hot and bothered, but this isn't the fun way if you know what I mean." Kimiko winked, then leaned her head on Blaine's shoulder. She murmured something I deliberately ignored in his ear, and his nose stopped spouting smoke. Mates tended to have that effect on each other.

"I think Kimiko won this round, you guys." I headed down the stairs to join the odd combination of Extrahumans near the food and drinks. All the untouched pizza just reminded me of Fred and how I wouldn't see him for almost a year. He'd gone off to the Under, also known as the Faerie realm. I sighed. My bandmates were cool and fun to hang out with, but Fred Redford was the guy I called when I had to talk about stuff like getting dumped. But Changelings have to pledge service to a Faerie monarch or lose their marbles. I'd have to get through this without Fred's help.

Even though I had a way better opinion of Tony than Blaine did, I would not talk to him about girl problems, either. The cat shifter was so agitated, he could have been a washing machine. The last thing he'd want to do was listen to me whine about Della and Jack. I turned my attention to the Psychic medium.

Bianca Brighton was the only person on campus whose hair color changed as frequently as mine. I had no idea whether that had anything to do with the fact that she saw dead people, dressed bohemian, or both. Everyone loved Bianca. She was almost the unofficial mascot of the Nocturnal Lounge. Even the folks who frequented the Solarium across campus had no beef with her. Maybe that had more to do with the aura of concern and sympathy that always seemed to surround her.

I didn't smile at Bianca, mostly because she hadn't noticed I was there. All of her attention was focused on what, to me, looked like an empty corner. Except I knew the truth; there were ghosts in the Lounge. Not because that was a given almost all the time at magical places, but because our resident medium wouldn't have been this intent on anything but a distressed ghost.

"It's okay, only I can hear you, and I promise not to repeat anything you don't want me to say in front of Blaine." Bianca sighed, her eyes bloodshot and the lids puffy. I sniffed as covertly as I could, and a faint tang of salt pricked my nose. She'd been crying. A low growl from my drummer told me he'd sensed the same thing. I knew he'd be confronting her about it, too. Pete always treated Bianca like a kid sister.

"Hey, Lane." Matt's elbow whacked me in the kidney. Good thing vampires like us don't need those. "Is that Irina Kazynski?"

I followed Matt's gaze up at the railing around the mezzanine.

Two women stood there, both raven-haired. One of them was tall, lanky, and looked like she could kick almost anyone's teeth in. The other one I'd know anywhere. I kept my lips closed over the smile that wanted to get all fangy and waved like a fanboy. I kind of was. Irina Kazynski was a Boston Conservatory graduate and internet-famous, after all. But even more important than that, Irina was good people. She'd risked her life in the Under helping Fred and his kid brother right along with me.

"Dude!" Irina waved back.

"You sound like Fred when you say 'dude,' man." I kept right on grinning, knowing Irina would get the inside joke banter I usually engaged in with Fred.

"You sound like a hippie when you say 'man,' bro." Irina headed down the stairs, holding out her hand to shake mine.

"Lane. Knows. Irina. Freaking. Kazynski." Matt took four steps back, then sat down in the chair he'd run into on the fifth word.

"Yeah. So?" Tony shrugged. "Great musicians are like birds. They flock together."

"That supposed to be some kind of insult?" Matt grumbled.

"Nope. Means you should make like a bird and get the flock over there, Matt. Hang out with the famous chick." Tony sipped his coffee. "But that's none of my business."

"Hey, Irina, these are Matt and Pete, two more of the guys in Night Creatures." I pointed at Pete and jerked my chin at Matt, who'd already gotten up to join us.

"Hi, guys." Her smile went flatter than soda left out all night. "Lane, we need to talk."

"Dude's all upset about plain old Della Dawn when a famous lady wants to talk to him." Matt rolled his eyes and elbowed Pete this time.

"Have some respect." I glared at my guitarist. "Fred's pledged all his deeds for the next year and a day to Irina."

"Oops." Matt put one hand over his mouth. "Sorry."

"Anyway, what's up?" I leaned against the banister.

"It's sort of about Fred, actually." Irina shrugged. "Well, kind of. It's about someone who helped us and a favor she asked for."

"Oh?" I wondered why Fred's debts had anything to do with me.

"Well, you remember how Ziggy the imp vanished you into the Under to help us, right?" Irina waited for me to nod, then continued, "They helped us because of a Summoner we met on the way in. Anyway, we maybe kind of promised that in exchange for her help, you'd let her interview you."

"Wait a minute." My stomach sank like the *Titanic*. "You don't mean Margot Malone, do you?"

"Actually, yeah." Irina grinned. "That's the Summoner I'm talking about."

"Oh." My face felt like that one time I'd taken a dare to eat a whole bag of Sour Patch Kids in under fifteen seconds.

"What's wrong, Lane?" Irina tilted her head, probably wishing she had her violin there or something. She looked pretty wistful about something, possibly someone. I really didn't want to say anything that'd make her mood even worse.

"Nothing," Matt answered for me. "Just that the Malone gal's been trying to interview Lane for about seven years now. He keeps blowing her off."

"Wow." Irina shook her head. "No wonder she seemed so thrilled with one interview in exchange for three summons."

"Wait. She gave you three?!" I blinked. Summoners needed years of training before they even got more than one creature to summon, and because of that, their services didn't come cheap. "How old is Margot Malone, anyway?"

"No idea." Irina chuckled. "And I wasn't going to ask. It's rude to ask a lady's age, even being another lady myself and all. Also, we were pretty desperate for any help we could get. We weren't about to look that kind of gift horse in the mouth."

"I guess I don't blame you and Fred." I sighed. "But did you guys really have to pimp me out like that?"

"I wouldn't call it pimping, exactly." Irina crossed her arms. "It's just an interview. What could possibly go wrong?"

"Oh, no." A trail of smoke wafted over from where Blaine had finally sat down with Kimiko in his lap. "Irina said the magic words."

"Yeah, we're in for it now." Kimiko rolled her eyes, then poked Blaine. The dragon shifter jumped, spilling his mate out of his lap. The Tanuki shifter landed on her feet, threw back her head, and laughed. "Well, Lane's in for it. And hey, Irina, what is this about a Summoner?"

"Why?" Irina raised an eyebrow.

"Ahem." We all looked up at the battle-ready chick in the mezzanine. That was Nox Phillips giving the stink eye to my bandmates. Not someone we wanted to piss off. She was a magical shifter, able to change into a horse and use water magic. On top of that, she had a black belt in some martial art I couldn't pronounce. "Peanut gallery. Beans. Unspilled."

"Oh." I grinned, not quite meeting her gaze. "Um. I kinda told them."

"Pardon my French, but *le sigh*." Nox shook her head. "I should knock you around a bit for that, but it wouldn't do any good now."

"Um, thanks, I think." I tapped my toe on the floor.

"Whatever." Nox waved one hand in the air, then sauntered down the stairs. I scuttled out of her way.

"So, can I tell Irina why we want to know about the Summoner now?" Kimiko jumped up and down, clapping her hands.

"Sure. Fine." Nox chuckled. "Just stop jumping up and down like you're in an anime being all *kawaii*."

"Aww." Kimiko pouted. "I thought I was in a book about a magic school being all Hermione Granger."

"Definitely *kawaii*." Blaine slipped an arm around her waist.

"As long as that's what you're into." Kimiko gave him a sly little smile. I blinked, wondering why the dragon shifter's wallet was in her hand all of a sudden. Then I remembered she was a Tanuki, and they always get caught stealing.

"Um, excuse me, but..." Irina put her hands on her hips. "I have a hanging question here. Suspense. Killing me. You understand, right?"

"Oh." Kimiko handed the wallet back to Blaine, who didn't even shrug as he put it back in his pocket. Must be nice, being a billionaire who could breathe fire, see magic and psychic energy, and turn into a dragon. And not care that his girl pinched his wallet. "Sorry, Irina. Anyway, we all know Lane is next, but we don't know who else is. If the Summoner's help got you through stuff neither of you would have made it past, maybe she's the other next person."

"Hmm, interesting theory." Irina shook her head. "But nah. I thought our little excursion to the Under debunked that whole two-target idea."

They were talking about a seriously powerful Extramagus who'd been attacking PPC students for some still-unknown reason. After Fred's adventure, the whole pack investigating the guy thought I would be next. With all the bad luck lately, it seemed likely.

"Maybe, maybe not." Nox poured herself some coffee, then stood where she could block Tony's chair from Blaine's line of sight.

"Well, all of you guys got targeted in mated pairs." Irina chewed on her lower lip. "But not Fred. It was him and his brother Ed who were targeted."

"That remains to be seen." Nox dropped a wink at Irina.

"Um. Fred and I met less than a week ago. Neither of us has ever even dated anyone before. And I still think he's a lunkhead. There's no way some Magus would think we're destined, extra or not." But Irina's usually pale face had gone crimson. She sure protested an awful lot.

"It's inconclusive at best." Blaine raised an eyebrow. "I thought I hated Kimi when we met for the first time, and just look at us now."

"Look, I don't appreciate you guys just deciding my future for me. Or destiny or whatever, either." Irina tapped one foot. Matt had a weird deflated look on his face. Relief? Dismay? Did he have issues with the whole destiny thing? I had no idea and no time to pry just then.

"I didn't appreciate it either when it happened to me." Nox opened her mouth to say more, but Kimiko shushed her.

"This is all beside the point, so stop giving poor Irina grief, mmkay?" Kimiko rolled her eyes. "It's not important, anyway. It has to do with help. Ed helped us indirectly, and Fred stepped up in a major way during that whole incident at Water Place Park. Irina, you did too, if I remember correctly. All I'm saying is, Lane helped Fred, Ed, and Irina. This Summoner did, too. Both of them in a Major League way."

"You don't think it's someone I care about, then?" I closed my eyes, picturing Della's face.

"I think maybe it could be." I hadn't noticed Bianca approaching. The medium was quieter than her ghosts sometimes. "And Lane cares so little about Margot Malone, he's avoided her for seven whole years, right?" She put her hand on my arm. "You must be worried about your ex-girlfriend."

"Wait, what to the who, now?" I pulled my arm away, freaked out for the first time by a Psychic. "I never said anything about exes."

"Della Dawn." Bianca blinked at something over my shoulder, then nodded. "It's a valid idea for sure, Horace."

"Your helper been following me, Bianca?" I narrowed my eyes. "And he's telling you everything that happens to me?"

"Yeah, well, everything he sees." She rubbed the side of one

17

hand under her eye, smudging her eyeliner. "Safety precaution. He came back here right after you left the Paragon. Jack Steele's an old-school vampire, too. Not like you guys, or others who got turned during the Reveal."

"Oh, I know." I rubbed my neck, on the side where I'd been bitten by whoever had turned me. But Bianca didn't need to know that.

"And neither are the Gatto Gang." Pete put his hands on his hips. "Did your little ghostie see that whole business?"

"Nope." Tony stepped out from behind Nox. "But everyone in here knows about that already."

"What? How?" I peered at Tony, trying to give the cat the benefit of the doubt. Blaine Harcourt didn't trust him, but I sure did. Or, at least, I had until the goons stopped us in the Trolley Tunnel.

"Because I told them." He sighed. "Paul and John flap their gums where I can hear them on the regular. I knew they were out there and looking for you guys."

"And you didn't give me a heads up, why?" I took a deep breath, trying to control my temper.

"Check your phone before you go ballistic on me."

I pulled out the device and the glove all vampires had to wear to use a touch-screen. Sure enough, there was a text message from Tony, right around the time we walked into Paragon.

"Well." I closed my eyes. "Isn't this a great big steaming pile of sh—"

"Hoo, boy!" The chirpy voice came from the platinum blonde with the Farrah Fawcett hairdo top of the stairs. She bounded down two steps at a time, nearly flying. I remembered this was Olivia Adler, an owl shifter. She leaned on the coffee counter, glancing at the space Horace occupied, then the corner Bianca had peered into earlier. But owl shifters couldn't be mediums. Was she seeing the ghosts or just guessing where they were? "What did I walk in on?"

Tony cut his eyes away, then hot-footed it up the stairs almost as fast as Olivia had headed down. I sank into one of the wing-back chairs, letting Pete and Matt tell the tale of my no-good, horrible, very bad night.

CHAPTER THREE

Band on the Run

"Are you sure we shouldn't be practicing our covers?" Pete spun on the stool behind the drum set, peering at the stiff Sidhe in the corner. "I mean, that's what we always get booked to do."

It had been almost a week of nights since Della dumped me and the Gattos made that offer we couldn't refuse. We'd gotten hold of Dave, our bassist, and he'd joined us for practice. He'd also canceled his trip to Australia.

"Yes." Sir Albert Dunstable, Sidhe knight in the queen's service, tapped the booklet he held, then adjusted his glasses. I'd been leery of his help at first, but he sure knew his way around any kind of rule or regulation. "It's right here in the rules that your original songs on the final night will count for the most points."

"We gotta do cover songs, too, though." Pete scratched his head.

"Yeah, but there's no way to practice for all of that in less than a month." I shrugged. "Besides, Pete's right. We're mostly booked as a cover band, and a pretty eclectic one, too. We'll just stress out trying to prep for all those decade categories." I glanced at Al. "How many were there again?"

"Ten, and no potential song lists." Al sighed. "You've got an excellent opportunity here, getting picked to fill in, but the timing is atrocious."

"I know." I sighed too. "But what can we do?"

"Practice?" The bounding sound of a strummed bassline came from the corner. I turned to look over at Dave, who peered out at us from over the thick black rims of his glasses. The bass player was all business most of the time.

I only nodded, slung my Epiphone's strap across my body, and stepped up to the mic. Pete twirled a drumstick, while Matt flipped his hair and wrapped his left hand around the fretboard on his Paul Reed Smith. I took a deep breath as the opening riffs filled the air, then sang the words to *Points*, one of our first post-turn originals straight out of 1999.

> *"Without a doubt, I knew it sucked that night*
> *We'll never win, 'cause no one thinks we're right*
> *We had to walk away and give up all our plans*
> *Why do I stop and turn around?"*

Before I could belt out the chorus, Matt slid his hand along the guitar strings. I turned to look, saw him staring at the doorway. I craned my neck to follow his gaze like I was watching a ping pong match. Irina Kazynski stood there holding the door open. Dave's funky bassline cut off, and Pete stopped his beat.

"Dammit." Matt hitched his guitar strap, so the instrument rode on his back, then stalked over to the mini-fridge. He grabbed a bag of blood and bit into it instead of bothering with a cup like we all usually did in polite company. I took note of the fresh rip in his otherwise ragged-on-purpose jeans and realized he had to be nearly crazy with hunger. No wonder he'd played like a maniac.

"Um, Irina?" I stood between her and Matt. "Now is not really a good time."

"You're right." She crossed her arms. "A good time to let Margot Malone interview you would have been yesterday. Or really any time since the night I told you about Fred's deal, maybe."

"Okay, I get it. But we have to practice, and having a human here is pretty distracting." I shot a glare at Matt. "For those of us who're too busy to bother filling up before practice."

"Um, but Al's sitting right there." Irina shrugged. "No one's biting him."

I sighed, not wanting to explain.

"I'm masking my scent and heartbeat with faerie magic." Sir Al to the rescue, go go Gadget chivalry. "You don't have glamour."

"I might not, but I can do this." Irina tapped her foot on the floor, her rhythm perfect, of course.

"Woah." Matt made a face and dropped the now-empty blood bag in the trash. "I'm not hungry anymore."

"Well, duh." Pete rolled his eyes. "You just had a bag."

"I needed more blood than that, though." Matt narrowed his eyes. "What are you, Psychic?"

"Empathy, dude." Irina tapped her nose in perfect time with her foot. Al laughed. Well, sort of. Guys that stiff and formal don't exactly laugh, they just chuckle without moving their faces, as if being straight-laced is social armor. And people think punks like us are weird.

"Well, I guess you can stay if you want to." I shook my head. "But I don't have time for interviews. We have less than three weeks to practice before the big event. We also have to worry about where we're staying."

"Yeah, our days of sleeping in the van ended the night we all got turned." Matt pulled his guitar back around and strummed a few chords.

"Let me worry about that." Irina chewed her lower lip, foot still tapping. "I have a couple of ideas." She pulled out her phone, then continued talking as she sent out a message. "Just worry about getting everything together musically. From what I heard out in the hall, you guys need the practice."

"What's that supposed to mean?" Matt stared so hard laser beams could have shot through Irina's face. He reminded me of a mean girl.

"It means all of you are off your game for some reason." She shrugged, leaning against the doorframe again. "You'll figure it out, though."

"Wait. What do you mean, all of us?" I knew perfectly well what had me distracted. Della. I didn't know exactly what was up with Matt. Maybe he'd joined a fight club? But he'd obviously been in a brawl, healed his injuries, and gotten hungry. "Pete? Dave? Is there something you guys aren't telling us?"

"Uh, well." The drummer scratched the back of his head, looking at his bass pedal.

"Spill it." I put my hands on my hips, trying to look authoritative. The neck of my Epiphone tilted down and whacked me in the knee. I winced. At least Pete was still looking down.

"I got an Incomplete. Got a make-up test to take." Pete glanced up, then away again. "Dunno how I'm gonna pass."

"We get you a tutor, that's how." I knew Lynn Frampton had helped Bobby Tremain ace a final he'd slept through all the notes for. I could see if she was available. "What about you?" I turned my glare to our bassist.

"Um, you know that trip I had to cancel, right?" Dave sighed, then dug his wallet out of his back pocket. He opened it and showed us a small photo of an attractive woman with a fanged smile.

"You sly dog!" Pete threw his head back and laughed. "The long nights weren't the only thing you wanted from Australia!"

"Well, I bet Natalie will never talk to me again now." Dave sighed.

"Didn't you tell her what's going on here?" I rolled my eyes. It all seemed so simple to me. "And that plane ticket. You could have swapped the destinations and put it in her name. Invited her here."

"What, to see us lose?" Dave put his hand over his mouth, his eyes wide behind his glasses. "Sorry, Lane."

"No, it's okay." I shook my head. "I feel the same way. And the only thing that will change our chances is practice, so let's shake off this funk and get it done."

A chorus of protests, mostly starting with the word "but," rose all around me. It felt like the time I'd been cornered and kicked around by an anti-vamp gang until the cops showed up. I almost caved and stormed out, but couldn't. The Gattos wouldn't let up just because Dave had girl trouble and Pete had grade problems. And Matt decided to act like Tyler Durden.

"You." I pointed at Pete. "I know smart people. I'm getting you a tutor. And you." I slapped Dave on the shoulder. "I'm calling this Natalie chick and making sure she knows I'm the bad guy here. And you." I glared at Matt. "Whatever your issue is, tell us about it so we can help. Otherwise, fix it yourself. If you don't, we'll have a lead violinist instead of a lead guitarist."

"Holy tough love, Lane!" Pete blinked. Irina snorted a laugh.

"Don't laugh, Kazynski." I crossed my arms over my chest. "You're coming to practice to learn our songs, just in case."

"Fine, but she won't need to." Matt gripped the neck of his guitar so hard I worried he might snap a string. "I'll deal." His fingers moved back into place, and he started the opening riff again. This time, we got through half our original material before the clock told us it was time to head home.

Five days later, Tony Gitano sat on the stool once occupied by Sir Al. Actually, he slouched. His face exuded boredom, but he kept tapping his feet to our music. I could tell we'd improved our performance on our originals even though none of us had realized how rusty we'd gotten at them.

The little red light on Tony's phone meant he was recording. I had no idea what he'd do with the video or audio recording and I didn't have time to care. Vampires with their feet to the fire shouldn't stand still, even when said flames were figurative. And I had to admit it might turn literal. The Gattos surely knew all the vampire weaknesses well. They weren't in the business of supernatural leverage for nothing. If Tony's dad wanted us to win, then we'd better. The last thing I wanted was getting our ashes handed to us.

I wondered for about the billionth time whether we could pull out a victory. Even though I hadn't known Jack Steele was a vampire while he taught me chords and time signatures, he'd always intimidated me. He was big, almost a bulky as Pete. The Gatto Gang had to have some enforcers who could put some hurt on Jack if they really wanted him to lose. But something about that idea bothered me. When we finished our new and improved rendition of Points, I called for a break.

"Hey, Tony?" I glanced at the phone and the red recording light.

"Yeah, what's up?" Tony tapped the screen and the light went out.

"Why are the, um, well, your dad's employees, um, well…" I wasn't sure how to phrase the question without sounding like I had a problem with Tony.

"You wanna know why the pressure's on you and not on Jack Steele and his egotistically named band." Tony raised an eyebrow, the ghost of a smirk on his lips.

"Yeah, something like that." I let out a whole lungful of breath I'd been in denial about holding.

"Too conspicuous." Tony tucked the phone in his trench-coat pocket. "Bad enough the band you're replacing has injuries. If the same thing happened to Jack or his dudes, the fuzz would get suspicious."

"Man, I can't believe you basically just called Newport's Finest 'the fuzz.'" I shook my head, snorting at the situational comedy.

"Fuzz, coppers, the po-po, bacon, blue-men group, whatever. And from what I hear, they're nice and cozy with old Jack. Too much heat in that kitchen." Tony waved a hand. "But I gotta ask, why are you changing the subject when you're the one who brought it up?"

"Thought you gave me an answer already." I shrugged.

"Ha!" Tony slapped his knee. "I got so used to Blaine Harcourt style interrogations about everything from my motives to my hairstyle, I guess I expect more prying. I'm a hinky cat-man, you know. Everyone in the Tinfoil Hat Pack is supposed to worry about whether they can trust me."

"Well, after what you did for Fred, I don't have that problem." I looked him right in the eye. "I trust you."

"Maybe you shouldn't." Tony met my gaze, not blinking or looking away. "That many brainy PPC Dean's Listers must know something, right?"

"They know plenty about books, research, and other academic mumbo-jumbo." I smiled. "You're not a course of study, man. I'm not all that sure why you let them treat you like one."

"I got no choice." Tony shook his head, finally cutting his eyes away. "They treat me exactly the way they should at this point. And I'm trying to tell you, copying them is a good idea. Walk the walk and talk the talk, even if you're faking it."

"I'll take your advice." I nodded. "Just don't forget that I'm doing it because I believe you."

"It's good to know someone on this plane of existence does."

Tony waved his hand again, this time in more of a shooing gesture. "Now, get outta my face, and act more like you're pissed that I might be spying on you. Because I probably am."

"Geez, Tony." I rolled my eyes. "Whatever."

I stalked back to my place behind the microphone, then counted to three. Night Creatures played on.

CHAPTER FOUR

Hotel Vampirella

"Welcome to the Hotel." The perky brunette with the high-neck sweater smiled, revealing nary a fang in her highly polished head. "What can I do for you?"

"Um, hi." I tried talking without moving my lips much. I didn't want to scare this lady, especially if she'd be got to decide whether we got room service or not. "I'm Lane Meyer."

"Oh. My. God!" The woman's perpetual smile got even bigger, a feat I hadn't thought possible. "I love that movie! The one with John Cusack and that awful young woman who dumped him for a skier."

"That's great." It wasn't. I hated that movie almost as much as the reminder that the protagonist I'd been named after while my mom was zonked on labor medication had gotten himself dumped, just like me.

"Anyway, here are your room keys." She held an envelope with what I assumed were four of those little plastic cards in it by one corner, dangling it between us like a dog treat. I understood.

"Gee, thanks!" I tilted my head to one side like the RCA mutt and tried to imagine a tail wagging behind me. "We sure do appreciate your hospitality here." I held my hand out under the envelope, glad I couldn't flush with anger at being treated like a performing lapdog instead of a sentient, if undead, person.

When she finally let the packet of keys fall into my waiting palm, I stifled a sigh of relief. If I had to act like a moron to get service here, I would. This hotel was the only place in Newport offering lightless rooms, not to mention the place Irina had arranged for us on the cheap. Which actually meant free. It was either stay here or dig a hole on the beach.

Luckily, the peanut gallery kept itself quiet enough to hear a pin drop. At least, they did until we headed down the flight of stairs to the basement and took a left to get to our rooms.

"*Welcome to the Hotel Vampirella*," Matt sang softly. I rolled my eyes. I didn't hate The Eagles. Who could? But who wants to contemplate the idea that their stay might go sideways?

"Yeah, okay, whatever." I tossed one of the keys over my shoulder. A slap of two hands coming together and lack of plastic clatter meant one of them caught it. While listening, I noticed something else. "Hey, we're not alone on this wing like we thought we'd be."

"Huh." Pete's hand came down on my shoulder, stopping my progress through the hall. "Sounds like a party's going on."

"Yeah." Dave stepped past me and jerked his chin at the door to my right. He was still bummed that Natalie hadn't come to visit. But, at least she hadn't broken up with him. "In there."

We all stopped, turning our heads toward the panel of wood marked 042. Sure enough, some music and a near-constant chatter came from the other side. I focused my aural attention on the rest of the hall, realizing the noise went farther than that. In fact, the entire even-numbered side seemed alive with sound. Life, too. I heard a gaggle of heartbeats.

I glanced down at the envelope in my hand, confirming that our room ended in an odd number. Good old 045. I turned my back on all the ruckus, found our door, and slipped the key in the slot. When the click came, letting me know the magnetic stripe had disengaged the lock, I pulled down on the handle. But it was too late. I growled. Then, I heard the door across the hall open. I turned.

"They're heeeeeeeeeeeeeere!" The lame *Poltergeist* quote came straight out of Lynn Frampton, standing in the doorway to 042.

"Oh, cool!" Bianca peeked over her head and waving at us all. "Horace says hi, guys!" She'd brought her favorite ghost on vacation.

"Hoo, boy, they finally made it." Olivia Adler yawned, rubbing her eyes before tugging at the hem of her pajama shirt.

"Move along, nothing to see here." Pete, Matt, and Dave got out of the way as Blaine Harcourt came down the hall with a keg of beer on his shoulder and another under his other arm. Lynn held the door open, then dragged an overstuffed backpack and a satchel out of the room after her.

"We're getting our study on, buddy." The brainiac tossed that satchel at Pete. His drummer's reflexes let him catch it even though he staggered back a step. "Irina's orders. You're turning that Incomplete into a passing grade. No excuses."

"Yes, ma'am." Pete nodded.

"Hey, dudes." A head popped out of the door to 044. I could hardly believe who I finally saw again.

"Hells bells!" I dropped my bags in front of the door to our room and stomped over. "Ren Ichiro! I heard you came back from the dead."

"Not really, just back from the greatly exaggerated rumors of my death is all." He grinned. "I'm a Selkie now, too. Water powers are spiffy."

"You and Beth married yet?" He'd been engaged to Josh Dennison's big sister before he vanished a few years earlier. The Dennisons were all werewolves, and with Ren sporting new magic shifter abilities now, I figured he'd be considered even more of a catch.

"Um." Ren glanced around, opening and closing his mouth a few times.

"Nope." Kimiko poked her head out from under her brother's arm. "Looks like I'm probably beating my dear brother in the Wedding Bell Invitational." Kim dropped me a wink and blew a raspberry at Ren.

"Can it, kiddo!" Beth's blonde head emerged from 046, her face wearing a scowl caustic enough to remove paint. "Your brother's not even in that race anymore." Ren sighed, vanishing back through the doorway.

"Hey, how many rooms did you guys rent, anyway?" I leaned against the wall, hoping all the noise would keep some shifters from overhearing my question.

"All of them." Kimiko smiled. "Well, the ones in this wing, anyway. We didn't want any, ah, trouble." She squinted at a spot just over my shoulder, and I remembered she could literally see Luck. "With your competition."

"Trouble?" I narrowed my eyes. "Why would you think there'd be trouble?"

"Don't worry about it." She flipped her hair over one shoulder. "It's just, when Irina called Blaine for a place to stay, she thought he'd be able to put you up at the mansion. You know, where it's warded."

"That's what I would have thought, too." I raised an eyebrow. "If we didn't want trouble, then why didn't he?"

"Hertha outmaneuvered him." Kimiko shrugged. "She gave some lame excuse about it not being a long enough time for decency after losing Wilfred."

"Wow." I'd almost forgotten that Blaine's stepdad had died. "I'm sorry."

"Oh, don't be." Kimiko shook her head. "Hertha isn't. She's milking the entire situation for all it's worth. Blaine hasn't even been allowed home since Spring Break ended. His mom usually goes overseas every summer, but not this time, apparently."

"Wow." I wasn't sure what else to say. My own parents hadn't given me any grief, doing huge renovations to make our house sun-safe once I got turned. They'd been awesome pretty much my whole life. I just couldn't get my brain around the idea of parents turning their backs on their own flesh and blood or making their lives harder. Maybe that was why I thought she must have had a reason. From the look on Kimiko's face, I shouldn't mention it, though. I was probably the only one in the group with that opinion. "Anyway, I'd better thank him."

Except when I looked around for Blaine, he was gone. So were the kegs. I closed my eyes for a moment, using my nose to try to pinpoint the dragon shifter's location. He was somewhere in the bank of connected rooms, but so were way more people than I'd expected.

"Josh, Nox, Irina, Sir Al, Olivia..." I opened my eyes. "Pure faeries?" I blinked at Lynn since Kimiko had gone back through the door with Ren.

"Yeah." Lynn grinned. "Gee-Nome's hiding in one of the bathrooms. There's a Pixie I haven't met, an imp, and heck, there's even a Spite outside in the garden. Irina calls them Daryl, but I'm nicknaming them Scaryl."

"Hey." I sniffed, realizing one scent was missing. "Where's Tony?"

"Oh, please." Lynn put a finger over her lips. "Don't say the T-word. Blaine vetoed him being here due to the risk of his temper causing him combustion issues. Fire is not good for the vampire complexion."

"But he's still coming out to watch us play, right?"

"Oh, yeah, our hinky neighborhood cat-man will be there." She nodded. "He's just staying someplace else."

"Okay, thanks." I wondered what place she meant, specifically, and then I imagined him sleeping on the beach. That just wouldn't be right. I figured I could call him and make sure, but not where Blaine could hear me. I headed down the hall, all the way to the corner where this wing met the other lightless one. And that's when I smelled her.

"Della." But no one was there. That other hall was empty and quiet. Well, not exactly quiet. I heard a low murmur from one of the doors. It was the same one with Della's uniquely appealing scent, and there was something else—some*one* else—in there with her. Familiar, too, but cold. "Jack."

Before I could head toward my friends or up the stairs to the lobby, that door clicked, opening to reveal my old music teacher holding an empty ice bucket and wearing nothing but a towel. I lucked out when he turned his back to me, striding down to the other end of the hall and the ice machine.

I'd never felt like such a chump in either of my lives, living or undead. Where I was lean, Jack was broad and muscular. Where I was lanky, Jack was built. And of course, I knew his musical talent surpassed my own without question. I might have been graced with the better vocal chops by Mother Nature, but his experience made even that one advantage tiny. Jack outclassed me in every way, and he'd ended up with my ex the same night she'd dumped me.

There was no way I'd win against him in any way, shape, or form. I was doomed; the Gattos could ash me once Night Creatures lost the Battle of the Bands. At least I wouldn't have to imagine Jack nude with Della if that happened. I headed up to the lobby and asked Siri to dial Tony. That AI was the best thing to happen to vampires with smartphones. No need to put on a glove just to make a call.

"Hey, Doctor Teeth."

"Hey, hep cat." The old joke greeting couldn't lift my spirits.

"What's wrong?"

"Just discovered Jack and Della have progressed well past the speed-dating stage."

"Oh. Well, that takes the cat box." Tony sighed. "It can't be that serious, right?"

"It's Jack-wearing-a-towel-to-the-ice-machine serious."

"Harsh."

"Yeah." I closed my eyes, trying to shake off the foul mood. "But enough about me. Lynn Frampton just told me you aren't allowed at the hotel."

"Yup."

"You got a decent place to stay?"

"Oh, I sure do." Tony chuckled. "I've got some friends in Newport who have nothing to do with the Harcourts."

"Really?" I hoped my skepticism wasn't showing.

"Truly." Tony sighed. "Look, I told you last week not to be too concerned about me or anything I say. No one else is." As it turned out, Tony was wrong.

"Um, Lane?" I looked up into a pair of big amber eyes framed by platinum blonde hair in a feathery cut.

"What's up, Olivia?" I pushed down the impulse to cover the phone with my hand. That wouldn't do any good. All shifters had hearing nearly as good as a vampire's.

"Olivia?" Tony actually gasped on the other end of the line. "Oh, no."

"That's Tony Gitano on the phone." She stifled a yawn. "I want to talk to him."

"Do *not* give her the phone." I didn't take Tony's advice. For some reason, I thought he needed all the goodwill he could get. And a blind man could have seen that Olivia cared.

"Hey, you're the one who said I shouldn't listen to anything you say." I handed the phone to the sleepily-blinking owl shifter.

I smiled as I watched her shuffle toward a comfy chair in the lobby's corner. Her slippers looked like big white paws. She sat down, chattering into the phone with a grin. Clearly, I wasn't the only one who did more than tolerate Tony. All the same, his recent behavior sure was suspicious. I couldn't even imagine what he might be saying on the other end of the line. Just as I was about to listen in, something bright green caught my eye at the front entrance.

I turned my head to see who or what came through the lobby door and my jaw hit the floor. A goddess in a kelly-green Mod-style dress swayed by. The woman had a face like an angel, curves to shame the devil, and hair like fire. If I'd been able to move, I might have been drawn to it like a moth to the most dangerous light source ever. But I was glued to my seat. Good thing, too.

All I could do was watch as the epitome of womanhood stood at the desk, one pointy-toed shoe tapping on the marble floor as she checked in. The lady behind the counter didn't play games with *her* key. Whoever she was, the redhead commanded respect. She certainly had my full attention.

My ears perked up as she asked for Irina Kazynski. Irina knew this vision of perfection? I wondered whether she could set us up on a date. The desk lady dialed the landline phone hovering over its number pad, waiting with me. Once Irina got up here, I'd have an in on their conversation. I willed my legs to function again. The last thing I wanted was to trip over my own feet on my way over to introduce myself.

"Irina!" My goddess held her arms out, reminding me of mannerisms I'd seen on 1960s sitcoms. I noticed the little pill-box hat perched sideways on her head. She was clearly into retro stuff. Maybe a vampire like me had a chance.

"Oh, thank goodness you made it." Irina took both of the redhead's hands, then turned her head. I caught her eye easily. "I have someone to introduce you to. Lane?"

"Hello there." I stood up and sauntered over, grinning and thanking the powers that be for the fact that vampires couldn't have sweaty palms. And I held out my hand. "I'm Lane Meyer."

"Oh, yes." The woman smirked, her eyes narrowing. Instead of shaking my hand, she reached into her little purse and pulled out a small notebook and pen. "It's so *good* to finally meet you in person." My stomach dropped at the sardonic weight she gave the word "good."

"Good to meet you, too, Miss," I glanced at Irina. "Um."

"Oh, this is Margot Malone." The violinist chuckled. I went from wanting to hug Irina to wishing the floor would swallow her. "You know, the reporter?"

Oh, I knew, all right. The knowledge that I'd been blowing off probably the most interesting woman in the universe hit me like a five-thousand-megaton warhead. I'd get to spend time with her, but she didn't exactly seem happy to see me. In fact, Margot looked distinctly unimpressed. She'd had to do major Psychic feats as favors for a shot at meeting me after seven years of mundane effort. I shouldn't be surprised if she ended up hating me.

"Hoo, boy," murmured Olivia from just behind my left shoulder. She tucked the phone in the left pocket on my flannel shirt. "Good luck, Lane."

I listened to the owl shifter's shuffling footsteps as she headed toward the lobby coffee machine. I remember thinking, maybe I should be the one to get swallowed up by the floor.

CHAPTER FIVE

Margot A Go-Go

"So, if you want it, I can give it to you right now." I instantly covered my mouth like an idiot instead of apologizing like a gentleman. I'd meant the interview, of course. But that wasn't how it sounded. Curse Freud and the slips he wrote books on.

"Wow, Lane." Irina shook her head. "And Fred told me you had class."

"When did he say a thing like that?" Margot looked down her nose at me.

"Oh, the other night, when you brought Ed and me to the Under for a visit." Irina shrugged. "You were there, remember?"

"I wasn't really paying attention." Margot nudged Irina with one elbow. "Figured a Knight and his Bard ought to converse without a vampire breathing down their necks."

"Yeah, I appreciate it." Irina smiled at Margot, offering her an arm. The redhead took it with a giggle. I blinked. I'd had no idea Margot and Irina had gotten so friendly.

"Well, I figured you'd need a break from Sir Al escorting you around." Margot rolled her eyes just before both ladies turned their backs to head down the stairs.

"Oy vey!" Irina chuckled. "It's like having a chaperon, visiting Fred with him around. How old is Albert Dunstable, anyway?"

"Oh, he's twenty-something." Margot's voice receded, but I couldn't stop myself from listening to her as long as I could. "Just from the most formal and stuffy Sidhe family in the entire state. Possibly even the entire eastern seaboard. Poor kid."

"He's the guy Lane had over to help the band learn the rules, you know." I heard Irina's laugh echo along the hall.

"Wish I could have seen that." Margot's voice sounded almost out of my range of hearing. I reached for the railing and took the stairs two at a time, intending to head after them even though I'd been blown off.

"Um, Lane?" I didn't recognize the soft voice behind me. I turned, stopping on the last step. A pale hand held my phone out to me. I took it.

"Olivia?" We blinked at each other, and the shine in her eyes increased as tears rolled down her cheeks, adding salt to her coffee. I'd never seen her like this and wondered whether her emotional state had to do with weaning herself off the meds that made her diurnal during school, or her conversation with Tony. Either way, it was probably none of my business, but there was only one way to test that theory. Ask. "What's up?"

"You're kind of in my way." She cut her eyes away, down to the marble floor or maybe my sneakers. And she was right. I'd completely blocked the stairs while eavesdropping.

"Oh. Sorry." I stepped aside, not sure what to do or say. But Olivia didn't move. She closed her eyes again, inhaling the steam coming off the surface of the liquid in the paper cup between her hands.

"I'm not talking about the stairs." She sighed.

"Huh?" I knew I was clueless, but this was ridiculous. "Well then, what is it?"

"It's Tony." She shook her head. "He says he won't talk to me again until this whole mess of yours is over."

"Wow, Olivia." I bit my lower lip, then winced, feeling like the lamest vampire ever. And I probably was just then, too. "I had no idea you and Tony were an item."

"We're not." She closed her eyes again, displacing more tears from the corners of her eyes. "Because he's a big scaredy cat. So we won't ever be if stuff like this keeps happening. And this time, it's your fault."

"Okay." I wasn't sure what she meant, actually, besides my Gatto Gang problems. I couldn't do a thing about the big bad Extramagus. At least, that's what I thought at the time. "What can I do to help?"

"Win." The word came out on a sigh. "That won't fix everything, but it'd be a start."

"Tall order." I felt like a piece of garbage. So many people—friends really or they wouldn't all be here—were counting on Night Creatures, and I was going to fail them by losing. "Jack's the most talented musician in Rhode Island, and maybe New England. We're gonna lose."

"If you think that, you will." Olivia stared at the band emblem on my shirt. "Because talent isn't everything in a contest like this."

"What do you mean?" I blinked. "It's not a vote, so you don't mean popularity. Besides, Jack's got that in the bag, too."

"Hunger." Olivia finally looked into my eyes. That word she'd uttered lingered in her gaze, but something in her eyes was distant, making clear that she wanted something or someone who wasn't here. "You have to want it so bad you can barely think about anything else. Jack and his guys have done this ten times. Count on their boredom. They'll underestimate how much you need this win."

"Believe me, Olivia, I've thought about how we have to win for weeks." I shook my head, wondering how she couldn't understand this. "But it's impossible."

"I'm majoring in Extrahuman Law. One thing they teach us is this: attitude is everything." The muscle at the side of Olivia's jaw twitched as she clenched it. Then, she took a breath. "If you believe you can't, you won't. Besides, you have three other guys going for this. Don't count their confidence out just because you're down on yourself over other stuff."

"Look, if you're talking about—" I stepped back, and would have toppled over if my epic vampire reflexes hadn't kicked in. "Ow!" Olivia had tossed her coffee at my face.

"I don't give two hoots about Della Dawn and her fang fetish, or that you think Margot Malone's hot and she's pissed because you blew her off for seven years." Olivia put her hands on her hips. I would never again forget that owls were terrifyingly perceptive predators.

"Um, okay." I put my hands up palms-out in a gesture of surrender. "So, what *do* you give a hoot about, then?"

"The people on the chopping block if you lose." She tilted her head and blinked. "Duh."

"I thought that was just me." I tried to shrug but my shoulders wouldn't move. That angry amber gaze had stopped me cold.

"What are you, new?" Olivia's nostrils flared. "Think about it. Who is Tony's dad? And where do you think a crime lord got the idea to put your band up against Jack's so he can game the inevitable gambling that goes with this contest every year? If the idea sinks, the guy who had it goes down with the ship."

"But Tony's his son."

"Did you know his dad shifts into a giant lion?"

"No." My mouth dropped open. I'd always thought fluffy little kitty cat shifters came from other fluffy little kitty cat shifters, not big lion men. "So, Tony's not heir to his father's throne, then?"

"Absolutely not." She shook her head. "He'll inherit a hole in the ground if he doesn't pull out some kind of gain for his family soon, too."

"Why are you worried over how he feels about you when he's told you all this?"

"Because he hasn't." She shrugged. "Owl shifters are some of the most observant people in the world."

"Holy Hendrix, you figured all that out on your own?"

"Don't tell Lynn." Olivia swished what was left of the coffee in her cup. "She'll start trying to compete with me academically, and nobody's got time for that."

"Okay. So I really have to win."

"'Have to' isn't good enough, Lane." Olivia's eyes narrowed until I wondered if lasers might shoot out of them. "I want to hear you say it."

"Huh?" I blinked.

"Say you're going to win." She tucked her chin, reminding me again of how scary owls could be.

"You're going to—" I stopped when she threatened me with the other half of her hot beverage. "I'm going to. No, *we're* going to win this. Night Creatures. Together."

"That's right, you are." Olivia turned her back and headed down the stairs. It wasn't the flounce I'd expected, either. It looked like a battle march. Even though Olivia looked and usually acted like a nerd, she had the heart and soul of a rebel. How else could a future lawyer be secretly infatuated with a Mafioso's son?

I headed to my room to practice instead of joining the party across the hall. We had work to do if we were going to win.

I'd needed that practice and the discipline that came with it. The next night, we stood backstage, glaring at the list of songs we had to choose from. For the first two events, both bands played covers in categories the judges chose.

"Well, here it is. Our worst nightmare." I passed the list

around, letting everyone see the title as I read, "Songs Played at the Disco."

"Suckitude," Pete grumbled.

"We're not a disco band," Matt growled.

"Guys, settle down." I stared at Pete and Matt until they shut their traps. Dave was a special case since he hadn't opened his trap. Instead, I waited through some sighing and a couple of eye rolls. "There's some funk on this list, too, so it's not just disco songs. Come on, Dave. We're not an Emo band either, so quit the soundless whine."

"But which of these are we gonna pick?" Dave took a deep breath but at least he didn't sigh it out this time. "I mean, do we all even know enough of them to make the set?"

"I know this one." Pete jabbed one big finger at the paper. He didn't make eye contact with any of us.

"Yeah, I do, too." Dave nudged Pete with an elbow.

"Same," I said. We all looked over at Matt.

"No freaking way." Matt's dreadlocks quivered like an E string wound too tightly. "I'm not playing that."

"But you know it."

"Yeah, but come on." He peered at me, head down like a bull about to charge. Matt was oddly uptight for a guitarist in a punk band. "You guys can't be serious. They televise this shindig. I don't want you implying those kinds of things when my mom's watching."

"Fine." I crossed my arms over my chest. "Find three more we all know." I heard Matt mumble something. "What was that?"

"There aren't three more." Matt shrugged. "I only know two on this list besides this raunchfest. This is the lamest contest ever, and unfairer than it is uncool."

"Well, we get a whole different genre tomorrow." I shrugged. "That's fair." I smirked, unable to stop myself from getting another dig in on my cocky guitarist. "Maybe it'll be Christian Rock."

"Yeah, man." Dave shifted his weight from one foot to the other. "Just think of it as getting the nasty medicine down. Or like eating broccoli before you can have dessert."

"Jeez, Dave." Matt shook his head. "You got turned when your brain was still twelve or something?"

Dave rolled his eyes, but I wasn't fooled. The bass player's lame analogy had been specifically designed to defuse the lead guitarist's ego trip. He'd been doing it for over a decade, since we all got turned. I mouthed a silent "thank you" to him over Matt's head.

We had our three songs circled, so we handed the list to the stage manager. It'd make its way to the judges. After that, we spent a couple of minutes waiting through the emcee's shtick before he announced us. As challengers, we got to go first, of course.

Just before we headed up the steps leading to the stage, a familiar, irresistible scent hooked me, pulling my head around to glance over my shoulder. Jack and his five bandmates stood in what passed for the green room back there. Della hung on his arm and I watched him tilt his head, clearly sniffing her hair exactly like I used to. Ew. I knew he could have been her great-great-grandpa. That thought process was more than a bit hypocritical, even though my age difference with Della only put me in older brother or possibly youngest uncle territory. I turned my head back, watching my step up to the stage.

Something coppery caught my eye—Margot's hair. She held a legal pad and pen like a shield and sword, jaw clenched with determination as though she were prepared for some necessary but undesirable task. I understood. She'd come to interview Jack. Of course, she wouldn't just be interviewing my underdogs and me at one of the biggest musical events of the summer. The Journal would pay better money for a bigger scoop. At least she didn't look particularly excited to be meeting Jack Steele. That made the way she'd shrugged me off the night before sting less.

Pete and Dave strode out on stage to scattered cheers. When Matt ran out, the crowd's energy and volume increased, with a number of wolf-whistles soaring above the lower-pitched hum and rumble. He was pretty enough to get mistaken for Lenny Kravitz back in the day. I could tell this was the biggest crowd we'd played to date. All the same, I wasn't ready for the wall of sound that greeted me when I sprinted out and across to my place at the front.

That was my natural element, so I stuck by the mic stand like a kid with his security blanket. A crowd that size required an attitude adjustment. The noise I smiled and waved into was like nothing I'd had directed at me in my entire existence. "Excitement" was too weak a word for the crowd's vibe, but "rabid" was too strong.

Inspiration hit me in the face like a bucket of water. I could have sat down and written an entire album about that feeling— the precipice at the edge of the chasm between small fry and big-time—but I couldn't write just then. I couldn't even improvise on a three-song set of covers. The trouble with being a creative and performing artist at the same time was that sometimes, you have to cut off your muse to please your audience.

So, I dropped my arm in the Night Creatures universal Start Playing hand signal. Dave responded by kicking in the bassline so Pete and Matt could layer the rhythm and melody over it. I strummed my chords and leaned in, ready to start the lyrics after the intro.

The crowd loved the raunchy funk song. One of the reasons we all knew *Love Rollercoaster* was the level of innuendo in those lyrics. The other was that we all grew up idolizing the Red Hot Chili Peppers, and they'd covered it. By the time we heard that song, the rumors behind that mysterious scream in the original version had been debunked.

Matt made the changeover from The Ohio Players to James Brown's sound look easy. It wasn't, but soon enough, I belted out the lyrics to *Papa's Got A Brand New Bag*. I wish I could have done the tune justice, but there was just no way a scrub like me could match the Godfather of Soul. The whole experience was humbling, especially when the crowd's noise morphed from roars to meows. I swallowed, remembering Olivia's warning about Tony.

And at first, when Pete and I laid off our instruments in order to let Dave and Matt carry us into the one ballad in the set, the audience went nearly silent. To this night, I still have no idea whether that came from boredom or anticipation. All I know is, after I set my guitar on the stand to my left and Pete finessed some percussion out of his high hat, the crowd had changed its mind.

It started with a whistle off to my right someplace, not in the front, but close enough for me to make out Blaine and Josh flanking Bobby, with Lynn perched on his shoulders. My less-than-stellar rendition of ABBA's *The Winner Takes It All* didn't flop, all thanks to the Tinfoil Hat pack.

But the assorted gaggle of extrahumans had nothing to do with the slow roar that started on the other side of the crowd. That was all Matt and me. When I got to the chorus and I sang about the loser standing small beside the victory that's her destiny, emotion charged our performance to high-voltage levels. I still wasn't sure what was going on with my guitarist, or why he'd come to practice most nights looking like something the cat dragged in. Whatever it was had to be hitting him harder than any physical blow that ripped his shirts and tore his jeans, though.

As we wrapped the song and the set, I knew we'd done better than I expected with what we'd been given. If it didn't turn out to be enough points to win, I had no idea what I'd do.

I also didn't know how to process the scene that met my eyes when we came down the steps backstage. Jack passed Margot a business card while Della pouted. Steele Ego and his band headed up to do their set. Della paced toward a corner and opened her handbag, refreshing her makeup and other girly activities I didn't care to watch.

Margot's actions were much more amusing anyway. She tucked the business card into a tissue and tossed it in a trashcan, then rubbed her palm on her skirt as though she'd touched something icky. That was fine and dandy with me. She gave me a full smile, fangs and all. If I'd been a creature of the breathing variety, I might have needed CPR. She opened her mouth to speak, but coincidence snatched whatever she'd been about to say away.

CHAPTER SIX

Watching the Detectives

"Lane Meyer." A woman's voice, as dry and practical as a laundress' hands, met my ears from someplace a little off to the right and behind me. "Can you tell me which of your bandmates was with you last night?"

"Um, sure." I turned to see a woman in a suit and shoes that screamed Law Enforcement. Her hair was wound up in a tight bun and slicked back, emphasizing the silver streak near the middle of her forehead.

"Oh, come on, Detective Weaver. Loosen up. You're backstage at a concert." The guy who stepped out from behind her looked much less professional in his puffy orange vest, acid-wash jeans, and mullet. Still, I knew he was a vampire right away. Older than me, too, judging by the clothing from my mom's early adulthood. "That's got to be some kind of romance-novel fantasy right there, huh?"

"Can it, Klein." Weaver snapped her fingers. "You know what we have to do here, and it's got nothing to do with romance."

"Yeah, doesn't mean I have to like it, especially not after a performance like that." Klein winked. Yeah, he was definitely the good cop. "That was freaking awesome. I always loved ABBA, and you guys killed it. I felt it right in here." He tapped his fist on the left side of his chest. I had no idea whether the detective was serious or pulling my leg.

"You feel nothing in there, Klein." Weaver rolled her eyes. "Detective business is serious business."

I blinked at the snark, wondering for a moment whether someone with more sarcastic chops than I had would think Weaver was the good cop. Before my contemplations could get any more like Dorothy Gale learning about good witches and bad, Klein grinned.

"Well, Detective Weaver is right, you know." Klein sighed. "We have some eyewitness accounts of you going into your room last night, but we don't know which of your bandmates were in there with you."

"Oh." I almost blurted that all of them were there, but that wasn't true. I didn't want any trouble with the law at a time like this, but that was all the more reason not to lie. "Matt, you weren't there. You left for a little while."

"Yeah, that's right." Matt nodded. "I went to take a walk and look at the water to clear my head."

"About what time was that?" Klein nodded and smiled, taking the goofy retro 80s vampire bit further than I'd suspected he could.

"Like, about eleven. I got back before two." Matt pulled out his phone and glove. "That's when Dave texted me about getting back for more practice, see?" He showed Klein something on the screen. Dave nodded, mumbling his assent.

"Oh, boy." Klein took a step back. "Well, Weaver. Looks like you're up."

"Matthew Gardner, you have the right to remain silent." Detective Weaver stepped toward Matt, holding out a pair of handcuffs. Margot put one hand over her mouth while Della stared. Pete grumbled something under his breath. Dave sat down on the stage manager's folding chair.

Jack Steele got back from his set just in time to see Weaver escorting Matt away. He blinked. After that, I thought I detected a small smirk on his face. I hung my head because we all knew the Night Creatures would never win this thing now. Matt was probably the only one of us with as much raw talent as Jack, and everyone knew it.

But then the corners of my own mouth twitched. They turned up right after, but I slapped my hand over my lips to hide it. Pete gasped, and Dave fell out of his chair.

Detective Klein was reading Jack his rights in a rote-memory almost-musical patois, snapping his own set of cuffs on my old mentor and new rival. Apparently, Newport's Finest had evidence against Jack more damning than anything they had on Matt. Jack didn't seem anywhere near as shocked and frustrated as Matt had, though.

I had no time to wonder why Jack's arrest left him unfazed. All the same, I wasn't sure what to do. But I knew full well who would. Tinfoil Hat.

"Come on, guys." I dragged Dave off the ground and out of the backstage area. "We've got people to see and plans to make."

Back at the hotel, I told everyone what had happened, and I mean everyone. Margot had followed us. Along with the wolves and other shifters were Albert the Sidhe knight and a particular Psychic violinist. Irina tapped furiously on her phone screen, and when I gave her a puzzled glance, she mouthed the word "Tony" over Blaine's head. I thought that was a good thing. Friendly neighborhood cat-man might have information we didn't.

"Okay, here's what's going to happen." Kimiko grabbed a tablet and started up LORA, the analytical app she'd designed to track local history and coincidence. She entered data as she spoke, making Lynn blink as she scribbled her own ideas on paper. "I'm handing LORA off to the other two brains here and heading down to Newport PD. Weaver and Klein wrote me some recommendations that got me into PPC the last time we dealt with them, so I'm going to offer them some help."

"Won't they think there's a conflict of interest, though?" Blaine puffed a smoke ring out of his nose. "It's no secret in local circles that I'm footing the bill for you guys." He gestured at me, Pete, and Dave. "And every society paper's been announcing our engagement for the last three months."

"That's why I'm going to help Klein with Jack Steele." Kimiko dropped a wink at Blaine, then leaned in and kissed the corner of his mouth. "Weaver's on her own, but Klein loves talking about his partner's exploits when he's playing teacher."

"You're brilliant." Blaine took the tablet his mate offered him.

"I know." The Tanuki shifter slung her handbag across her body. "I'll be in touch. Expect at least one data sync over LORA from my phone during the next few hours."

"Wait for me." I hadn't noticed Olivia grabbing her own bag. "I want to be in the right place for Matt's bail hearing in the morning." The owl shifter turned around, then grabbed an amber bottle that rattled in her hand out of the nightstand drawer. "I'll need these."

"Oh, that sucks." Nox shook her head. "Thought staying in town for the summer would give you a little time off the diurnal meds."

"Who else can do this lawyer-lite stuff on such short notice?" Olivia tapped Blaine on the shoulder. "We need Al in case of faerie problems. And Blaine, how much bail can you afford?"

"Not much, unfortunately." More smoke trailed from Blaine's nose. "My dividend check's almost gone, and last time I talked to Mother, she said she wasn't helping me until I apologized for disrespecting her about Wilfred."

"What?" Lynn's notebook and pen clattered to the coffee table. "Bobby and I'll march over there and give her hell for you, Blaine." She stood up, and Bobby stepped up beside her as he cracked his knuckles.

"No way." Blaine's nose stopped its smokestack imitation. "No one deals with Mother but me."

"When the time comes, though," Bobby narrowed his eyes, "you won't have to deal with the dragon lady alone."

"I know." Blaine replied to Bobby, but he looked past him at Kimiko. It struck me that Tinfoil Hat was a formidable pack, mixed and misfit bag or not. I could barely believe they all were on my side. "What about you guys?" Blaine glanced at Josh and Beth.

"Yeah, I've got a similar issue." Josh wrinkled his nose. I'd almost forgotten that their family was more than just respectably well-off. "My grades dipped last semester, so my folks cut me off until I show some academic improvement."

"And with me going back to finish school this fall, I'm tapped out." Beth sighed. "Sorry."

"Look, worst-case scenario, if there's not enough to bail him out before the next set, I'll fill in for Matt." Irina patted her violin case. "I know they have a magic and psychic dampener onstage, but that degree from The Boston Conservatory has to count for something."

My shoulders came down from my earlobes. Well, not literally, but the tension in them sure did ease. We wouldn't have to forfeit the Battle of the Bands if they held Matt during the next part of the contest.

"I'm loving this pack solidarity and everything," Josh said, holding up his phone, "but we have new information." He nodded at Kimiko and Olivia, who stood near the door to the hall. "It'll all go into LORA, I promise. You two go and do your thing."

"New information?" Lynn ducked past Bobby to peer at the phone in Josh's hand. "From Henry?"

"Yeah." Josh tilted the phone so Lynn could see. Her face flushed a shade of crimson I mistook for embarrassment. "I'll share with the room, but it might be better to do this first. Hold on a sec."

The Alpha wolf sauntered over to Blaine, then tapped his phone against the tablet. The latter device made a chime reminiscent of GLaDOS from *Portal*, giving me a better idea of Kimiko Ichiro's nerdy sense of humor, and then LORA spoke. Well, kind of.

"Compiling data. Cross-referencing. Coincidence detected." A red glow lit Blaine's face from below, reminding me of kids telling ghost stories around a campfire. "Watkins brothers connected to Extramagus activity over four decades."

"Tiamat's scales!" Blaine jumped up off the sofa. "Do you know what this means?" I didn't, but I was in the minority, along with Dave and Pete.

"Yeah." Lynn leaned back against the cushions. "It means we've got nothing. Professor Watkins is in a vegetative state, and his brother's been missing since the Reveal."

"Well, we can still find at least one thing out about those guys." Bianca Brighton stood in the doorway to one of the connecting rooms.

"How?" Josh shook his head. "We've had all our researchers on this, and there's nothing in official records. If there's anything else in Henry's memory trinket box, it'll take weeks for him to get. Even our man on the street hasn't heard any rumors."

"I can find out whether they're dead or not." Bianca sighed. "Even if they've moved on, I know plenty of ghosts who've been around long enough to remember seeing them before that happened."

"Why do I get the idea there's a catch here?" Josh put his hands on his hips.

"Because there is." Bianca leaned her back against the door

frame. "It's not easy to contact that many unfamiliar ghosts. Takes a lot out of me."

"Well, is there any other way?" Josh raised an eyebrow.

"Nope." Blaine shook his head. "No other way to deal with ghosts than to get help from a medium. And you need a ghost who was a medium while alive, too."

"Right. A ghostly medium. Your friend Horace is one of those, right, Bianca?" Nox rubbed the bridge of her nose. "At least, that's what I remember from when he chatted with my dad and Wilfred." I blinked, suddenly realizing why Blaine had been at the Nocturnal Lounge the night this all started. Bianca had been talking to his stepdad.

"Yeah, that's right." Bianca closed her eyes, then stood and stepped over to the mini-fridge. She opened it and took out a zippered case. "I'll need about twenty-four hours and protection, though, because I'm going to be totally out of touch with the living world. Also, someone has to test my sugar and give me this if I need it." She unzipped the case, revealing a glucometer, a collection of dainty syringes, and a vial with the word Humulin on the side.

"On it." Lynn took the case from Bianca.

"And I'll do the physical guarding in there." Bobby followed the ladies back into the room Bianca had come from. "None of us will be in the crowd to cheer you guys on tomorrow, but this is important."

"Thanks, guys." Josh closed his eyes, then opened them again after the door between rooms shut. "Ren, get out in the hall and guard that door tonight." Josh clapped the Selkie on the shoulder. "Nox, I want you out there during the day tomorrow."

"I'll make sure nothing gets vanished in except the food and drink they'll need." I looked down because the voice came from so close to the floor. A tiny, pot-bellied creature with what looked like dentures made of shark's teeth smiled up at me.

"Thanks, Gee-Nome." Josh nodded at the Gnome. "I appreciate your help, especially with Henry and Maddie up in Vermont all summer."

"The Watkins brothers are my friends, too. How do you think I met Henry in the first place?" The Gnome winked at him, then vanished with a pop of displaced air. That made no sense to me. Everyone else looked confused, too, so I shrugged off Gee-Nome's odd comment.

"Do you want a pure faerie guard with your magical shifters? I can send a Seelie for Ren and have one switch off with Gee for Nox." I blinked at the sound of Margot's voice.

"Why are you helping?" I'd figured her earlier anger was a matter of vampiric principle, but I had to wonder whether I should question her motives.

"Because I pissed off this Extramagus, too." Margot put her hands on her hips. "And the whole blood-loss thing reeks of a frame job aimed at vampires. If I hadn't had an alibi from interviewing Irina, I'd be in the slammer, too."

"Yeah, Margot helped Fred and me with something major in the Under, like I told you already." Irina folded her arms over her chest. "Didn't I say I thought she's his other target? Did you forget that or something?"

"No. Well, yeah." I sighed, then looked Margot right in her amazing emerald green eyes. "Sorry, Margot. About everything."

"Just give me that interview I've been waiting seven years for within the next couple of days, and we're square."

"Sure." I got up, walking toward Margot, fully intending to make good on that promise right then and there. Then my phone rang, and the course of my night changed.

CHAPTER SEVEN

My Father's Room

"Hi, Mom," I said into the speaker. "What's up?"

"Lane, it's your father." Her usually quavery voice shook even more with fear. "He's trashing the nursing home again."

"Sorry, guys." I went directly out the door. "Family stuff."

As I headed down the hall, I heard Pete and Dave telling everyone with better-than-average hearing that I was used to handling this particular problem on my own. They were right, but I sure would have loved some company. Outside the hotel, I breathed a sigh of relief, realizing the place I was staying was only a couple of blocks from the facility Dad had lived in for the last handful of years. I'd dashed out without asking for the keys to the van, and the irony of my absentmindedness was like a punch in the gut.

I turned up the street, my strides eating sidewalk as fast as I could manage without letting on to the hipsters and other vacationing folks that I was a vampire. In less than five minutes, I approached the front desk. I knew the lady seated behind it, a mortal retiree who worked here on the overnight shift.

"Hi, Jan." I showed her my Extrahuman Registry ID, and she wrote its number down with a V beside it, indicating I'd voluntarily disclosed my vampiric status.

"Yes, hello, Jan." I froze at the feminine voice, staring down at the ID pushed across the desk by a delicate, manicured hand. A head of wavy red hair framed the woman's face in the picture, green eyes twinkling even in the captured image.

"Margot?" I turned to look her in her actual face. "What are you doing here?"

"Thought you could use some company, even if you've got things covered."

"You mean an alibi, right?" I raised an eyebrow, not wanting to go into detail about the police and the Gattos in front of the nice lady who'd been checking me in and out to visit Dad all this time.

"No, I mean company." Margot closed her eyes and sighed. "I've been in places like this too many times." I peered at the birthdate on her ID, which read September 18, 1949. She opened her eyes again, meeting my gaze. "But if you'd rather go alone, I'll head back to the hotel."

"Um, Jan," I glanced back at the desk attendant and almost did a double-take because her eyes were all misty. "Uh, is it okay if I bring Miss Malone with me?"

"Of course." Jan nodded once firmly. She dabbed the corner of one eye. I wondered whether Jan was Psychic or something. If she was, I didn't want to know what she just saw. "As soon as I get her signed in."

Jan did the paperwork while I tried not to stare at Margot. This gorgeous, brilliant woman understood about combative elderly folks with dementia? And I'd been the idiot blowing her off for seven years. "Idiot" was too weak a word. I'd been a colossal jerkwad, assuming a lady like Margot Malone was some fangirl band groupie with a lame 'zine or blog.

We walked through the double doors after Jan buzzed us in. I let my feet travel the familiar route. The only silver lining to Dad having Alzheimer's and being stuck in here was that I never got lost in places like this anymore. Neither did Margot, apparently, even if she did pause in front of the wrong door for a moment. But there I went, making assumptions again. Maybe it wasn't the wrong door, just the wrong time for it.

Margot had a quiet and subdued quality I hadn't seen from her before. That could have been a symptom of our limited interaction, but only a blind man wouldn't notice that the sparkle in her eyes had dulled to practically nothing. Something about this place in particular had her pushed farther down than I usually dared to tread. A strange lightness welled up, buoying me along with it. I refused to let her flounder alone.

"So, I want you to be ready to duck." I nudged her arm with an elbow. "Quack, quack."

"Duck?" Margot blinked.

"Yeah." I grinned, and her lips answered with the halfway kind. "Dad's got Telekinesis."

Her mouth made a little round O and her eyes went wide. They glittered inquisitively, that sparkle back. I smiled. She looked away, seemingly at nothing just as we turned the corner into Dad's room, then Margot promptly tripped over a fallen picture frame. I caught her, of course. Vampires don't have epic reflexes for nothing. I felt like a big hero at that moment instead of dragging my zero-sum self-image behind me like a ball and chain. That tiny rescue unshackled me for once. I wanted to get used to the feeling.

"Lane?" Dad scratched his head, which was partially obscured from view by the collection of objects hovering in the air around him.

"Yeah, Dad. I'm here."

"Well, it's about time." He shook his head like it weighed as much as his old '57 Chevy SS. A can of shaving cream bounced in the air near his left shoulder, bumping into a black plastic comb. "You almost missed your curfew again."

"Sorry, Dad." I shrugged, wondering why my shoulders and arms didn't move much. Then I remembered—Margot still rested in them.

"Well, you made it. Come on in, you two. No need for me to tell Mom you cut it close." Dad shrugged exactly the same way I did. All the objects lifted for a moment, then settled again into their holding pattern. Dad had used his Telekinesis as an entertainer, making hundreds of people happy every night back when he was my age. Well, not my actual age, but the age I'd look forever. Twenty-three.

"Yeah, Dad. I did." I'd gotten so much from him, and this damn disease kept taking all our common pieces away one by one. I blinked, then felt a touch on my cheek, surprisingly soothing and cool.

"Lane?" Margot's fingertips came away damp.

"Yeah?" I managed to keep any more tears behind my eyes.

"Aren't you going to introduce us?" She turned her head and grinned at my father.

"Oh, yeah. Of course." I set her down beside me, then stood up straight. "Dad, this is Margot Malone. Margot, this is my dad, Ken Meyer."

"Hello." Dad moved a bottle of Listerine away from his stubbly face, peering at Margot like a bird who'd found something shiny. He was all there for that inspection, too. The vacancy that made regular appearances in his eyes as the disease progressed was out for the moment. "How long have you and Lane been dating?"

"Oh, tonight's the first time we've gone out together, Mr. Meyer." She cocked her head to the side and then giggled. "But I've been interested in seeing him for a long time."

"Really?" When Dad smiled, it was like some of the light in Margot's eyes caught on in his. I couldn't remember seeing him this happy since we had him out for the day on his and Mom's fortieth wedding anniversary. "And what are your plans after high school?"

I froze. I'd known from the beginning that Dad's Alzheimer's had him doing a Time Warp. One of the reasons Mom always called me in was the coincidence that made it so I'd always look like he remembered I should. I acted like it too, but that part was on purpose. If Margot corrected Dad, all his toiletries would go flying, likely at her face, and I couldn't warn her not to without setting him off.

"Oh, a couple of years at college, then an internship." She grinned. "I'm going to be a reporter. Thanks for asking, Mr. Meyer."

"Please, call me Ken." My dad brushed past his toothpaste, his aftershave, and a bottle of Old Spice and took Margot's hand in both of his. Then, he turned his head, looking me right in the eye. "Hold on to this one, sonny boy. She's a keeper."

I stood there, watching silently as all of Dad's toiletry items floated gently back through the bathroom door to their proper places around the sink. He puttered around, offering Margot some tea and saltine crackers from his bedside table. She declined, of course, telling him I'd taken her out to dinner. After that she fell smoothly into the patterns and patter of pretended mortality in a way that reminded me of Jack. She had something in common with my rival; both had lived as vampires before the Reveal. I'd never have managed. I sucked at pretending.

When Dad told me he'd better go to bed, and to come back right away after walking Margot home, I knew the nursing staff wouldn't have any more trouble with him that night. He shuffled off into the bathroom, running the water as he loaded his toothbrush with paste and tumbled mouthwash into a tiny cup.

On the way out of the room, Margot picked up the picture she'd tripped over, setting it on the dresser by the door. She grinned softly, then took my hand as we entered the hall. She didn't hold it long, just enough for a reassuring squeeze. It felt strangely empty when she let go. After that, she busied herself with her handbag, doing nothing in particular with the strap.

I waved at the nurses, listening to our footsteps making hollow sounds in the hall like water knocking against the hull of a small boat. And I went through the motions of checking out with Jan, tucking my ID away in my pocket instead of bothering with my wallet. Then I waited just outside the door until Margot emerged before heading back to the hotel on the deserted street.

"How did you know?" I couldn't look at her, afraid for some reason that something about her would blind me, be as impossible to gaze on as the sun. "How did you know to just roll with it like we were seventeen?"

"Because I've been there." Margot's voice was flatter than week-old soda. She didn't say anything else. I let her clam up for almost a block.

"Do you want to talk about it?"

"No one ever asks a reporter questions."

"Well, I just did." I shrugged, then winced as I thought about Dad and me and how, if I hadn't gotten turned, I'd get to look forward to a life like his down the road. I felt like the world's biggest cheater. "Because reporters are people too. You don't have to answer, though."

"I know. And maybe that's why I will." She took a deep breath. "It doesn't get better, you know. It just gets farther away. My mom was in there, ten, fifteen years ago. She thought I was seventeen, too. After a while, she thought I was her sister. Near the end, before she lost her speech, she thought I was her mother. And then, she was like an infant. I came here every night once that happened. But she didn't last long after."

"Mom can't calm him down." I shook my head. "Do you think it's because he's not seeing her? I mean, really seeing, I don't know, *her*? Like he saw you and me?"

"I don't know. Maybe that's a question the doctors will be able to answer someday." Margot had a little shake in her voice. This time, I dared to look at her. And she was nothing like the sun. The tears on her face gleamed like diamonds or maybe stars. This time, I was the one reaching for them.

When I dropped my hand, she took it again. If I'd been really alive or had the energy to pretend I was, I might have blushed or flushed. Even though I wasn't, my stomach contorted itself into knots. All the same, I felt an odd sense of calm in all the storms of dealing with such mortal problems.

CHAPTER EIGHT

I Only Drink Blood

I'd just stepped out of the shower. Yeah, vampires shower. We end up smelling like wherever we've been if we don't, and Long Term Care Facility wasn't my jam. I sat in the chair all hotel rooms seemed to have, the straight-backed kind they put in front of the desk, with a seat that looked cushioned but wasn't.

The notes pouring from Irina's violin would have made me sit down if I hadn't already been on my keister. I'd heard her fiddling before, of course. In person, too. But listening to her play one of our original songs along with Dave and Pete had an entirely different effect. I'd written this whole song before the Night Creatures even formed, except the guitar solo. That had all been Matt's creation, and it was Irina's one weak point. She could handle the covers, but with the Night Creatures' original work, it was mimicry of the most technical kind.

The worst part was, I knew what kind of musical magic Irina could do. I'd heard her up close and in person, pouring her heart and soul out through her instrument. And here she was, not doing that because she knew the stage would stop her Empathy from affecting the audience. I stood up, about to try putting the lyrics into the music, hoping that'd wake whatever part of Irina all that fire came from. The phone rang, and I almost snapped it in half.

"Lane?" I waved at the others to stop playing, then put the call on speaker.

"Yeah, Olivia?"

"Matt's still in jail. His bail was super-high."

"That's totally unfair!"

"I know. I tried telling the judge that Matt wasn't a flight risk because of the contest, but she didn't want to hear it."

"What about Jack, though? If he's in there too, maybe the contest will get postponed." I wasn't sure the Gattos would like that, but at least I could argue that the Jack Steele Band didn't win.

"But he's not." Olivia's voice sounded jittery, more like what I recognized from during the semester than how she'd been over the month since I'd helped Fred in the Under and gotten more directly involved in the whole Tinfoil Hat pack and its Extramagus woes. "Jack got released on his own recognizance."

"Well, I'll call the Battle of the Band judges and let them know that—" Pete smacked his palm to his face, which snapped me out of the automatic and incongruent response I'd been in the middle of. "Wait. You said Jack is not in jail?"

"That's what I said." Olivia sighed. "I can call Mr. Ichiro and see if we should look into a discrimination case since Jack's white and Matt's not. That'd take months, though."

"Well, that's just amazeballs, with an extra helping of awesome sauce on top." It wasn't. "I'll tell Matt to talk to Mr. Ichiro some other time."

"Sorry, I'm just lawyer-lite instead of the real thing." Olivia's words had Irina frowning and shaking her head.

"Hey, you actually tried helping a literal band of vampires." I nodded at Irina, glad Olivia couldn't see how close I was to tearing up. "You're the coolest lawyer-lite owl-girl I know."

"Tell it to the cat." Her words had my head jerking back in confusion.

"Isn't the saying 'tell it to the judge,' though?" I scratched my head.

"Yeah. Sorry. These meds wreck my brain." I heard her vaguely hooty yawn come across the line.

"Listen, get off the Ritalin and catch a nap, okay?"

"Yeah, okay. Sorry again, Lane. Bye." The phone beeped as she disconnected. I closed my eyes. When I opened them again, I said, "Take it from the top again."

This time, when they did, I joined in.

Hearing me sing and play rhythm guitar along with the others the second time through had done the trick. For a while there, I'd been worried Irina just didn't get what our music was about. She'd spent four years in Boston, after all, only reluctantly coming back to Providence and facing her extrahuman past because her grandpa needed help. Finally satisfied with the practice, I'd been about to call it quits and tell our non-undead understudy to go get some sleep. But when I took a breath, something happened.

It was like the night I'd been turned after I blacked out. I'd caught a scent from out in the hall apparently, because when I came to my senses, that was where I stood. The wheels on the room service cart squeaked like nails on a chalkboard at the far end of the hall. I took one step toward it and the service elevator it waited for. At least, I thought it was only one step.

I was next to the bellhop, a lady in red and black I'd never met before. She looked nothing like Della Dawn, but the scent coming off her was all my ex-girlfriend and more. My mouth was open, fangs bared, head bending toward her as she stood with her back pressed to the still-closed elevator door. She wore a name tag. I only know because I remember smelling the nickel. Everything in that moment was scent and the rush of this woman's rapidly increasing heartbeat.

My teeth clicked together when the fist met my jaw. The punch would have killed me if I'd been alive. As it was, it broke my neck. I couldn't bite anyone like that unless they fell on my fangs. The pain had killed my appetite at any rate. I heard another smack and crack as I toppled to the garish paisley carpet.

Above me, Nox Phillips was putting her foot down after connecting it with the back of Dave's head. My usually reserved bassist snarled, diving at the bellhop again until Nox landed a chop across his jaw, dislocating it. He went down across my legs with a grimace.

Nox continued her movements, as fluid as a dancer but a million times more lethal. Watching her spar with Pete was like watching an old wire-fu movie, except real and wireless. I remembered that they'd both trained at the Cherry Blossom School, and it looked like awesome sauce on both of them. Pete had those enhanced vampire reflexes, but Nox was another kind of creature altogether. Her hair was slicked back with water, which meant she had her Kelpie pelt on. The enchanted item gave her extra strength, speed, and water magic straight outta Faerie. She'd also have been able to shape-shift and trounce Pete with no trouble at all, but the hall was too small for horses, magical or otherwise.

Pete's palm struck Nox in the chest, and she went down. He covered her, going straight for the throat. Shifter blood tastes gamy, but by that point, Pete's hunger had taken over. A blue light, faint under the fluorescents overhead, surrounded Nox, and the carpet got soggy and slick a moment later. Then an enraged howl filled the hall and my ears.

A blur of fur, fang, and claw knocked Pete askew, slamming

the drummer into the room service cart. Something about that bothered me, but I couldn't place it. At least, not until the elevator dinged. My eureka moment came with the sound. Silver. The cover on the cart was made out of that, with a handle in the shape of a star. I could smell it, just like the nickel name tag.

The woman my band of hungry vampires had attacked scooted into the elevator, her finger pressing the button repeatedly creating a tattoo of clicks. Pete's foot slipped as he lunged at the Kelpie, and his face hit the carpet instead of her neck. A white-furred blur glanced off his shoulder, tumbling into the toppled cart, cover and all. I smelled even more gamy shifter blood before hearing the too-human scream.

"Josh!" Nox kipped up, kicking Pete in the neck just to be sure he stayed down, then rushed to her mate. I made a mental note not to piss her off again if I was sensible enough to help it. Kung-Fu Kelpie knew what to do when it came to fighting vampires. She also knew enough to dial 911 immediately when werewolves got impaled by sterling silver.

"Woah." I sat up, even though my head was at a totally wrong angle. I'd never seen a wolf shifter knocked out of his animal shape by getting wounded with their metal bane. It seriously sucked. "I'm sorry, guys. This is all my fault."

"Not your fault." Josh winced as he rolled over, holding his side. The blood oozing from between his fingers smelled rancid now, like he had an infection but worse. "That woman smelled funny."

"Yeah, but not literally." I winced, trying to get my hands around my neck to pop it back into place before healing it with blood power. "I don't know what it was about her, either."

"You'd think a hotel that caters to vampires would vet their employees better." Dave rubbed his jaw. "She smelled like the best thing to drink in the universe."

"Crap on a crap cracker." I stared at the phone, only half-listening to Nox stating the nature of her emergency. "We're about to get even more police attention."

Sure enough, Detective Weaver showed up on the heels of the paranormal paramedics. Josh had ordered Sir Albert to watch Bianca's hotel room door before passing out. I'd have bet all three hundred bucks in my bank account that he'd thought Nox would be too distracted, but not enough that she'd get in the ambulance with him. Weaver took her phone number, and I hoped she'd use it before arresting another of us. Our injuries *were* illegal, after all.

"So, what happened here?" Detective Weaver tapped the round toe of her "obvious cop" shoe. Her partner, Detective Klein, wasn't there, of course. He was a vampire just like me, and it was high noon out there.

"Um." I yanked again at my head, desperate now to make my neck right again. I felt like a moron, forgetting to insist on help from the paramedics before they left. "That nice young lady who went with her mate in the ambulance beat us up."

"Oh really?" Weaver tilted her head, that white streak in her hair shining in the dim light of the claustrophobic hall. "Nice young lady, huh?"

"Yeah, and we deserved it, too." I told her how the three of us vampires had ended up outside our room, noses telling us there was something delicious out here.

"I suppose the real question I should have asked you is, are there any human witnesses besides the one who's upstairs with her boss trying to stave off a nervous breakdown?"

"I'm one." Irina leaned against the wall opposite Detective Weaver. She smiled to shame the Devil, too. I was surprised until I remembered she'd made the exact same face at the Sidhe freaking Queen just a month before. To Irina, a cop like Detective Weaver must seem like small potatoes.

"This story of Mr. Meyer's—is it accurate? Complete?"

"Not exactly." Irina shouldered up from the wall and put her hands on her hips. "Lane and the other guys probably don't remember this because vampires who riled up aren't all there, as I'm sure you know." Irina pulled her phone from her pocket, tapped, swiped a few times, and held it out to the Detective. "I've got something better than my memory, though. I'd been recording our practice session and caught something else. Have a listen."

Detective Weaver tapped the phone one more time. I listened to my voice repeating the same word over and over before hearing a terrified feminine screech and then all the noise from the fight. I would have tilted my head, but my neck was still borked.

"Well, that's interesting in a Confucian sense. Lane Meyer calling Jack Steele's girlfriend's name." She snorted. "Sounds like tabloid fodder." Detective Weaver gave Irina back a grin to rival her earlier one. "I'm taking your phone in for evidence."

"Yeah, fine. Sure. Whatever." Irina shrugged, reminding me for all the world of Fred. "Do what you gotta do, ma'am."

"I'll help." Kimiko Ichiro stepped around the corner. Margot followed a moment later, tucking a notepad in her bag.

"Get all of that recording and the one preceding it." Detective Weaver handed Kim the phone, then turned her back to head off down the hall. "If there's anything from the concert last night, I'll want that, too. And enhance it all until I can hear Meyer's nose hairs vibrating when he hits the high notes."

"Yes, ma'am, right away." Kimiko nodded and pocketed the expensive device like a good little Tanuki shifter. Before she turned to follow the detective, she dropped me a wink. If the police had to investigate, at least we had the sneakiest member of Tinfoil Hat looking out for us.

But none of that would help if we flopped at that night's performance. With Josh and Nox out of commission, I wasn't sure we'd be safe from the Gatto goons, either. I eyed Blaine, standing next to Albert outside Bianca's door. I wasn't sure I wanted to know what Kimiko would find on that phone. What I wanted was to talk to Tony, but couldn't with either the sun or Blaine Harcourt glaring down.

I shuffled toward my room after Dave and Pete. When I got to the threshold, a slender hand, familiar in its soothing coolness, met my shoulder.

"You've got a little problem there, Lane."

"Yeah." I awkwardly turned to try to look at Margot. "This whole day's been a giant pain in the neck."

"Vampire karma." She smiled. Her fangs looked nearly as diamond-like as her tears had before. Had our walk back from the nursing home really been less than twelve hours earlier? It felt like forever and only a moment at the same time.

"Well, what can you do?" I tried a shrug, but it wasn't very effective. I felt like a weak Pokemon.

"Fix it, of course." Her smile got brighter. "If that's okay with you?"

"Yes. Please, fix it." At that moment, I would have sworn on everything I cared about that Margot Malone was an angel, lack of wings and fangy smile notwithstanding.

"Okay. On the count of three." She put her hands on either side of my face. "One." She placed her thumbs in the hollows of my cheeks and tucked her fingers against my jaw. "Two."

"Ow!" My neck snapping back into place felt like a car crash and sounded like a sawed-off shotgun. "Thought you were gonna wait for three."

"You might have flinched." She unwrapped her hands from my face. I tried not to lean forward or moan. It was a near thing. Her touch felt better than Della had ever smelled. I had no idea why or how, just that if I tried saying anything, it'd sound pathetic.

"Fair enough." I tilted my head from side to side. "Thanks, Margot." I had the feeling I'd been saying that phrase so much she might get sick of it.

"You're welcome." She turned on her heel and headed down to the other end of the hallway. I had no idea why until she pulled a key card out of her handbag and unlocked the door.

As she turned her head to smile at me one more time and give a tiny wave, something bothered me. Margot must have been working on a story in the basement lounge. Any human would expect her to be in her room at noon. I shivered, wondering whether there was a reason the bloodthirst-inducing employee had been right outside her door. Who would be trying to get Margot Malone in trouble? The Extramagus, of course. And that made me angrier than any of the crap he'd thrown my way, too.

CHAPTER NINE

Meyer, Meyer, Pants on Fire

We weren't even in our room for fifteen minutes before someone knocked on the door. I'd laid down with my arm over my face, so I didn't get up. Instead, I groaned a string of words that basically meant "go away." But then, they knocked again, louder this time.

"No. We gave at the office," I called out, louder and more coherently this time. They. Knocked. Again. Those. Jerkwads. I got up, stalked to the door, and flung it open with fangs bared.

"Um, excuse me." A squeaky voice came from somewhere near the floor. "Um, could you put the sharp pointy teeth away, please?"

"Uh." I looked down. A tiny blue-skinned creature dressed in what looked like a tunic made of silver fish scales gazed up with eyes like spotlights. They were a pure faerie—a Pixie, if I wasn't mistaken. I scratched my head and blinked. The last time I'd heard of a Pixie was from Fred.

"Hi, my name's Nixie." The creature blinked back, fidgeting their feet in something like a soft-shoe routine. "Should have said that first, sorry. Oh, and can I come in? That's a thing with vampires, right? Needing to be invited in? I always get it mixed up, even though I'm friends with one."

"Sure." I chuckled and stepped aside. "We're the ones who need an invitation, but only for actual homes. You could have barged right in."

"Well, that'd be rude." The Pixie crossed their arms over their chest, then took a seat on one of the spokes on a guitar stand. "So, I bet you want to know why I'm here."

"Um." I glanced around for Dave and Pete. The shower was running, and a faint rustle came from the bed at the other end of the suite. Only Pete moved in his sleep, so that meant Dave was in the bathroom. "I could assume this information is for my ears only. Or I could wait for the others."

"No, just you." Nixie rolled their eyes. "It's about Della."

"Della. Um."

"Yeah, you remember Della, right?" The pixie shook their head with a chuckle. "You should remember your ex-girlfriend."

"Of course, I remember her, silly." I flipped my hair over my shoulder. "I'm just wondering what a nice Seelie faerie like you is doing with dirt like that."

"Oh, I get all sizes, shapes, and textures of dirt." They winked. "Comes with the territory when you hang out with a reporter."

"Oh!" If I'd been sitting, I would have stood up. As it was, I bounced on the balls of my feet like a weird Punk Elvis impersonator. "So, you're friends with Margot."

"Well, it started as a working relationship, but yeah." Nixie smiled. "She's the kind of person it's hard not to get friendly with."

"I hear you." I took a couple of steps backward, then sat on the floor to chat with the little creature. "Sounds like working for Margot's a pretty good deal."

"Uh, I'm here to tell you something about Della, though." Nixie narrowed their eyes. "Hey, wait. Do you have a crush on my boss?"

"What kind of question is that?" I smacked my forehead, realizing I'd better watch it with the questions around a Pixie.

"The kind people ask when you change the subject from the potentially life-saving information I've been asked to deliver to chatting about a bubbly redhead." Nixie sighed and rested their cheek in one hand. "I need to tell you this stuff so I can get on with the really important things in my day."

"Okay, lay it on me." I wondered for a moment what Nixie the Pixie might have on their schedule, then remembered Fred's stories. This faerie probably had tickets to a musical or something.

"Della is freaking out. Has been since yesterday. She's been looking for something that went missing from the hotel room after the night you all got here." Nixie sighed. "She thinks someone on the hotel staff took it, and after today, so do I."

"Wow, Nixie." I blinked. "It sounds like you're as smart about figuring this kind of thing out as some of the folks across the hall. There's got to be more, or you wouldn't still be hanging out here."

"Yup, that's right." The Pixie couldn't look me in the eye all of a sudden. "I'm supposed to tell you that Jack's been biting her."

"What?" I stood up and rushed to the door again. Della might not be my girlfriend anymore, but biting a living human was illegal anywhere except on private property. Hotel rooms didn't count as that for vampires. Jack could get arrested again and solve all my problems with winning the Battle of the Bands and the Gattos. But biting humans after getting involved with blood-doll rings back in the day was bad news. Jack could kill her if he wasn't careful. "That piece of—"

"Still Waters." At the faerie's words, I was immersed in something, like my arms and legs moved through taffy instead of air. "Lane, you can't go and confront Jack. He'll just deny it. And anyway, Della's happy about the biting. Some humans like that sort of thing, and you know it. In fact, it has something to do with her missing item, whatever it is. You want to find out what that is, right?"

"Sounds like a job for Newport's Finest, not a Punk front man."

"I thought you had a little agreement with a certain group of big cat shifters." Nixie stepped around in front of me and smiled up. "You call the police back after that whole tangle out in the hall, it'll look awfully suspicious to them. Weaver and Klein already know those Gattos are here, too. They're trying to figure everything out, and that's not good. The last time Detective Weaver crossed the Gattos, bullets flew. It got worse than that, later on. Just ask Blaine sometime."

"So, what do you and your boss think I should do?" I'd already heard about the night Blaine, Kimiko, and Jeannie got shot at, Mafia-style. I definitely didn't need to deal with anything like that.

"Get some of those friends from across the hall and look into it yourself." Nixie clapped their hands, then stuck them out to either side with the fingers spread wide. Jazz hands. On a pure faerie. I'd heard about it but never thought I'd actually see it.

"Sure, fine, okay, whatever." I shrugged, my shoulders and arms moving normally in the regular plain old air this time. Apparently, those jazz hands released the Still Waters spell the Pixie had hit me with.

"That's super peachy-keen, Lane." Nixie headed toward the bathroom door, which had just opened. A bewildered Dave in a fluffy white hotel bathrobe and foggy glasses did a double-take when the Pixie dashed underfoot. I heard a rush of water as I chased after them. The bathroom was empty, but the faucet in the sink trickled cold water.

"Was that a Pixie?"

"Yeah." I tossed Dave's t-shirt and jeans at his face, then headed across the room to where Pete slept.

"What did they want?" Dave pulled his clothes on under the bathrobe, locker-room style.

"They want us to drag our lazy behinds out of bed and give some info to the brainiacs across the hall." I flicked Pete in the temple. "Get up or your head's going in the bass drum again, dude."

"Harsh." Pete sat up, rubbing bleary eyes. "I've never even seen a Pixie, and already I don't like 'em."

I grabbed some bags of blood from the mini-fridge, then opened the door and headed across the hall. My bandmates came after me. Before I could knock, the door opened. Blaine stood there, looking sleepier than Pete.

"Go on in." He stepped aside and stuck his arm out, palm flat like some kind of host at a restaurant.

The suite was a mess. Crumb-dusted pizza boxes fought for counter and table space with empty bottles and cans. Blaine plopped on the sofa with his tablet. He tapped it to wake it up.

"I'm going out on a limb and assuming you guys came over here with some information for me."

"Yeah, we did," I told him most of what Nixie had said.

"Tiamat's scales!" The air around Blaine's head got smoky.

"Hoo, boy!" Olivia stepped out of the bathroom wearing jeans and a t-shirt, her "lawyer-lite" outfit draped over one arm.

"Yeah, I know." I shook my head. "Even more things suck than we thought."

"I wonder what Della's missing?" Olivia adjusted her glasses. "And what Nixie thinks it has to do with your hall brawl."

"Do you rhyme all the time?" Pete rolled his eyes at the owl shifter.

"Oh, come on." I sighed. "Look, we have big trouble ahead."

"Yeah, and it's so bad, someone could end up dead." Olivia smirked.

"No more rhymes, now. I mean it!" Blaine's smoke came with a little extra heat this time.

I wasn't sure whether I'd start hitting something or roll on the floor laughing if anyone offered Trogdor a peanut. I didn't get a chance to find out, either. Nox came back right then, with Albert the Sidhe knight in tow. A yawning Ren shuffled past to take his place guarding Bianca's hall door.

"What's the word on Josh?" Blaine turned that smoke into a pretty ring, just like the ones he used to make during less stressful times at the Nocturnal Lounge. I guess he wasn't continuing the rhyme-time madness by himself.

"He's in the hospital, sleeping. Silver poisoning." She curled up in a chair, reminding me more of a cat than a chick who turned into a magic horse. "Gonna be a couple more days before they release him, too."

"So, this sucks. We don't have our Alpha or our Beta. Someone's got to sub in and act as one." Blaine shuddered, then put his finger on his nose. "Not it."

"I'm too new to the group to qualify, I'm afraid." Albert shook his head, a hint of a smirk on his lips as he leaned against the wall.

"Dammit." Nox's finger was poised to tap the tip of hers, but she'd been too slow.

"Anyway, I'll give all this new information to LORA while I fill you guys in." Blaine retold my story almost verbatim. I wondered whether he had a naturally perfect memory or if it was a dragon thing.

"This Della," Albert said, "she was your paramour? What drew you to her?"

"Um, the way she smelled. It's what I noticed first about her, but that's supposed to be pretty typical for vampires."

"I'm aware." He toyed with a lock of his long platinum hair. "But just over an hour ago, the three of you attacked a woman. Why?"

"She smelled delicious." Dave's comment made me blink. He

usually clammed up in front of people he didn't know well, but he had come out and said the thing I hadn't been able to.

"So, Della's got an attractive-enough scent to hook a guy who's played the field since 1999." Blaine blew a smoke ring. "She loses something important to her at a hotel with her new boyfriend, who she's convinced to bite her despite it being illegal. And then, a staff member working on the floor where she's staying smells delicious." Blaine grinned. "I think we've found our answer, folks. I'll bet dollars to donuts Della lost some special perfume."

"Yeah, the magical kind." Nox ran a hand through her hair. "That stuff's not exactly legal, but it's pretty popular with a certain type of girl."

"Wait a minute." I shook my head. "That can't be right. I never tried to bite Della even once."

"Well, maybe she found a different magic perfume after she started dating a different guy." Olivia shrugged. "I don't know much about magic cosmetics, but if Lane never wanted to bite her and she wanted to be bitten, doesn't it make sense for her to look for a boost?" The owl shifter glanced down, her face reddening. "It's like wearing a push-up bra to get a guy's attention. If it doesn't work, some girls might try the kind with water, even though those have a risk of embarrassing wardrobe failure."

"Been there. Done that." Nox nodded. "Threw away the t-shirt. But it's magic perfume. Hmm, I wonder if coincidence has anything to do with it? Lane didn't make a habit of biting people because he got turned after that was the way all the vamps did it. Jack's older, so he's more likely to bite."

"I've got nothing." I shrugged. "But it sounds like you ladies know way more about this subject than us guys do.

"New data shows a pattern in vampire-related crimes." LORA's creepy voice actually made me step back. "Coincidence detected for subjects Lane Meyer, Peter Hartford, Matthew

Gardner, and David Goldberg. Same witness detected at all scenes."

"Give us the dates, LORA," Blaine said.

A thud to my left and a gasp to my right meant Pete and Dave had both reacted. But I couldn't, left more immobile by the revelation than Nixie's stilling spell. I should have known the whole situation felt familiar, and I should have known LORA would spit out today's date, along with the date of the night we'd all been turned. The other two dates she gave in January rang a bell, but I didn't know right away how they related to us. None of us could move. I could barely think. Fortunately, we got by with a little help from our friends.

"Bianca? You awake in there?" Nox headed to one of the suite's connecting doors, which was closed, and knocked on it.

We all waited in silence as the door unlocked and opened, revealing a sleepy-looking rainbow-haired Bianca Brighton in flannel pajamas. She tilted her head, listening for something. Her eyes went wide at whatever she heard, then she dashed into the room and snatched the tablet from Blaine. Lynn and Bobby peered out after her.

"Ooh. Oh, no." She shook her head. "Lane, please tell me exactly what the vampires who turned you guys looked like."

"Uhm. Uh." I hemmed and hawed so much I could have been a sewing machine. Pete lowered his face into his hands. Dave hunched his shoulders and stared at nothing. "I don't remember. None of us do."

"Crap on a crap cracker." Blaine sighed heavier than all the funky stank bass Dave had laid down on stage the night before. "And Henry can't help you remember, either. He's in Vermont."

"Maybe Horace and I can help with this." Bianca beckoned me toward the small breakfast table by the suite's kitchen.

"What's this about?" I sat down.

"That witness LORA mentioned is Professor Nate Watkins." She sat across from me and leaned her elbows on the table, reaching her hands across. "He's the reason no one pressed charges against you and the other guys when you got turned. He heard someone talking about spiking your drinks and making you irresistible to vampires so they'd turn you."

"Really?" I couldn't look up after Bianca blurted the details I hadn't told anyone. I couldn't handle the disgusting truth that we'd been turned against our will any better seventeen years after the fact than the night it happened. All four of our lives had been taken, but the nature of vampirism left us all lingering, and I'd been trapped in a continuum of depression and angst the whole time. All I could do was stare at the mottled manmade marble top of the hotel breakfast table. It was green with black flecks. I'll never forget it. I'd never forget Tinfoil Hat's reaction, either.

"Dude. That sucks." Ren Ichiro crossed his arms over his chest and scowled through the doorway. "We can make things even worse for whoever did that to you guys."

"Yeah, literally and figuratively." Blaine's nose puffed out even thicker smoke.

"And I thought I couldn't get any more pissed off." Lynn's teeth ground audibly. Bobby's answering growl rose in harmony with his mate's anger.

"Someone should cut off all their legs." Beth's usually open face twisted in a snarl. "I volunteer as Tribute."

"As long as I'm Tribute from another District, Beth." Nox cracked her knuckles.

"Honorable combat is too good for that sort of miscreant." Albert's right hand went to his left hip even though he wasn't wearing his sword.

I could have cried and almost did. Pete sniffled to my right. I turned and saw him sitting on the floor with Dave crouching nearby, the bassist's face wet with tears even though he didn't make a sound. Whatever higher power had dreamed up vampirism and denied us enjoying food while giving us the near-constant thirst had at least left us with the ability to cry about it.

"Okay, then." I turned to look at Bianca again. "What do you and this Horace guy have in mind?"

"Well, LORA mentioned related crimes with coincidental connections and all. She's tracking stuff related to the Extramagus." Bianca grinned but her gaze stayed steely. "If Professor Watkins witnessed all of them, all we have to do is figure out what that connection is, and we'll have enough evidence for the police to take the guy into custody. We won't have to do this on our own anymore."

"It seems like a whole crowd of people besides Night Creatures cares about this." I shrugged. "So, how do we find the right connection if LORA doesn't have it?"

"Mediums like me are the only living folks who can see and hear ghosts, but we can also communicate with other incorporeal people. I've been talking to all the ghosts Horace can find, trying to track down the Watkins brothers. So far, we haven't found them, which means they're not dead." Bianca pressed her lips into a thin, pale line. "It means Professor Watkins is out of his body because that's his Psychic ability—Projection. We know where his body is, so I'll be able to talk to him with a bit of extra effort. I'll need some information from around here, too, but this is all connected to something that affects you personally. I won't do it unless you're all okay with that stuff getting brought up again."

I nodded. "Do it." Pete and Dave mumbled their agreement.

"Okay." Bianca stretched her lips in a thin smile. "I need to borrow Pete for about an hour at sunset." She headed for the door, my drummer following. "Come on, Horace," she said to thin air, "we've got more work to do."

CHAPTER TEN

Good Song Hunting

"Nineties songs?" Pete snorted. "We've got this one in the bag."

"Don't be so sure." Dave pushed his glasses up the bridge of his nose, then sighed and took a few deep breaths to focus his Psychic energy. "We have to read that list and be ready to pick something different if The Jack Steele Band takes one of the songs we wanted to do."

"It sucks that they can't just tell us which ones they picked." Irina straightened the spangled vest she had on over a shirt that looked like it belonged at a Renaissance Festival. "That reeks of unfairness."

"It wouldn't be much of a battle if we knew." I shrugged. "Besides, they had to change one of their choices when we did that James Brown number last night." I shook my head. "I can't believe that was only twenty-four hours ago."

"Yeah, I know." Pete skimmed the list, running a finger down the paper. "Hey, how about a little GNR? A violinist will tear those guitar solos apart."

"I'm down for that." Irina smiled. "What else?"

"Why don't you pick one this time?" Dave shook his head violently, testing the Telekinesis that kept his glasses on.

"Okay. I wanna do that Spacehog one."

"Are you serious?" I blinked, wondering how she'd pull that one off.

"Yeah." She nodded. "It's a challenge, but I've been working on my own cover of it for YouTube. Fred's doing the vocals, but he's on a Quest right now, so I don't want to get rusty on it."

"That's two songs in the bag, then." Pete smiled. "Pick one, Dave."

"This bites." He sighed. "There's no Chili Peppers on this list. Were the judges even listening to music in the nineties?"

"Dunno. Maybe they thought it'd be unfair." I shrugged. "Would you really want to risk battling with Peppers songs, anyway? Jack has an upright bass."

"That gave them an advantage on all those songs from the disco last night." Dave scratched his head. "Okay, I have it. That." He tapped the paper with one finger.

"Good choice, but we should cut down the extra choruses and some of the instrumentals." I jotted some notes on the back of the sheet. The others nodded. I knew they were all solid enough to make the changes. "The crowd will love that one, and with Irina here, we can totally pull it off."

We listened to the Jack Steele Band up there, making the crowd go wild. They'd picked popular songs, every choice a number-one hit. They'd decided to cater to the audience, who had mostly grown up listening to music from the nineties, but they had no fire in their performance. During lessons, Jack had always told me how mediocre and baroque recent pop music was. He'd refused to teach me with it, telling me how the raw bones were more important than that ubiquitous wall of sound.

I shut my eyes, remembering. If the judges had gone a decade earlier, we'd have lost this round before we even stepped onstage.

Jack had taught me on post-punk because it was so bare and intense. My hands curled as I pictured myself back in his Pawtucket basement apartment, making the chords for *Love Will Tear Us Apart* by Joy Division. I shook off the memory but kept the melancholy that always followed those lyrics. I'd need it if we were opening with *November Rain*.

But we couldn't. We had to scramble to choose another song because that jerkwad Jack decided to close his set with it. I kept my eyes shut, listening to them bicker.

"What about this?"

"No. No Marilyn Manson. I can't stand them."

"Okay, then. How about this?"

"I mean, we could try it, but I don't know anything by Train."

"Give me that." I opened my eyes and snatched the list from Irina. "Here. We'll do this."

"I can't believe he picked that one." Pete's eyebrows went so far up, I thought they'd merge with his hair. "Are you sure you can handle it, Lane?"

"I can sing anything, mofo." I flicked his ear. "Even that one."

"I don't know, Lane." Irina's face was crinkled like she'd just sucked on a lemon or something. "Maybe I should sing it. I mean, contextually, it's going to be super weird."

"Why?"

"Uh, because you're a guy?" Irina made a grimace that was probably supposed to be a grin but had an extra helping of awkward.

"I'm a vampire." I flipped my freshly touched-up green hair, throwing all my weight on one foot and striking a pose worthy of Posh Spice. "And I'm Lane fracking Meyer. I'll sing what I want. The rest of you guys had better punk up the music, though."

"No problem!" Dave actually pumped his fist in the air, practically hyperactive compared to the laid-back bassist demeanor he usually affected.

We ran up onstage, waving. Once Pete was behind the drum

set where he belonged, we got right to it, starting with Irina's pick, *In the Meantime* by Spacehog. The crowd went nuts. I thought Jack had made a mistake by only choosing songs by American bands.

I'd always imagined the lyrics were a message from an outside species to the human race. As a vampire singing them to a largely human, or at least mortal audience, it felt truer somehow. I put my arms out, as though I could somehow hug that crowd, and serenaded them with the sentiment about loving them all in the meantime. Their applause hugged me back.

I let Irina lead into the next song, beginning what would have been a piano intro at a Meatloaf concert. She nailed it better than a carpenter at a construction site. When I started singing, the violin floated under my voice like a breeze does when you put your hand out a car window into the slipstream. Singing about what I'd do for love and what I wouldn't felt like smelling coffee, or maybe a dash of cold water to the face. It woke me up, and I understood the song. Finally.

When Irina belted out the lines in the bridge, it almost conjured Fred to my mind. The only reason Irina Kazynski wasn't a front man was that she was a front woman. She had to know what it was like, having groupies looking for a memory or a story to tell at parties. Fred had decided to dedicate every heroic deed he did in the Under to her, and she'd accepted that. Now I knew why. Every performance needs a specific audience— someone to pitch it to. And there was no better person to devote the rest of this contest to than Margot Malone. She had become my proof there could be life after undeath.

Maybe that dedication and not the fact that I was Lane fracking Meyer as I'd bragged was the reason song number three ended up rocking so hard. I had realized its potential, and it made me achieve liftoff. Pure joy, the contagious kind, bubbled up from my center for the first time in what felt like ages. *Bitch* by Meredith Brooks turned out to be the jewel in the crown of our set.

When I sang about being a sinner and a saint without being ashamed, I thought about how everyone was each of those things at some point. The song wasn't particularly brilliant, but that was the way of popular music. Stones have to be tumbled, cut, and polished if you want them to shine. We'd found a diamond amongst the quartzes and jaspers and managed to put our own sparkle on it.

The applause was like thunder, even in that outdoor venue. I held my arms up, waving, then bowing, seeing Irina salute the crowd with her bow and Pete clapping his drumsticks together. Even Dave bounced around, hugging his bass and not worrying about whether his glasses stayed on. I tried saying thanks into the mic, but the sound techs had already turned it off.

When the lights dimmed, I cried. Matt hadn't been there, and he should have been. I headed off the stage, the other three trailing behind me as I wiped my face on my forearm. When I lowered it, I smelled something delicious. No one was there, though. Irina ran right into me, and I fell on my face. The stiletto on a high-heeled shoe almost ran my eye through. I gasped, then turned my head, looking for someone to help me up.

"Well, this is a huge surprise." The familiar voice wasn't the one I wanted to hear. In fact, it was one I'd just as soon never listen to again.

"Paul. How's it hanging?"

"Way lower than you'll be." The Mafioso's mouth tilted down at the corners as he stomped over to me. "Would you look at this, John? Our boss decides to help Lane out, and he goes insane. Does a crazy thing like icing a dame. The odds ain't ever in your favor no more."

"What the fu—" John's fist introduced itself to Dave's jaw before he could get the other half of that word out. My bassist hurtled backward into an instrument rack.

"And after that brilliant performance, too." Paul shook his head, clicking his tongue against his teeth a few times.

I saw Pete take up a fighting stance, relieved to see he might kick more than a bass drum tonight, but then something flew out of John's hand, hit Pete in the chest, and stuck there. A stake. He fell on his back in front of me across something that made a smack instead of a thud and released more of that delicious smell from before. I opened my mouth, unable to stop myself from baring my fangs. I glanced back at the shoe, noticing the foot in it this time.

Irina screamed, then lifted her violin. That was the only thing that saved her. John and Paul both had their hands on the butts of the pistols in their shoulder holsters. The notes pouring out of Irina's instrument weren't soothing. She couldn't have managed that while facing off against two hardcases who hadn't even touched their shifter forms yet. Instead, her music inspired abject terror, primal and startling—a feeling like standing in front of a jackknifing eighteen-wheeler.

Paul turned tail and ran, and John grew a tail. Flight and fight in the same duo; what were the chances? Unfortunately, Irina couldn't fight John now that he was a fear-fueled half-ton lion. John roared, his tail twitching as he crouched in front of the violinist. I shouted for help.

"You need a miracle!" The new voice was familiar too, but such a relief. An imp stood between the Roman lion and Irina Kazynski, their little hands held out on spindly arms. "Scat!"

The imp snapped their fingers, and the lion shifter vanished with a pop. Irina stopped playing, and Dave groaned. I pushed up from the floor with my hands.

"Wow, thanks." I grinned at the imp. I'd met them before, of course.

"Don't mention it." The imp smiled, tugging their fake beard.

"Margot sent you, Ziggy." I blinked. I'd almost forgotten that she was a Summoner as well as a reporter.

"Yes, and she paid for your miracle, too." Ziggy snapped their fingers again and vanished.

"Um, Lane?" Irina stood with her back against the rail of the steps leading from the stage. She trembled like water when someone threw a stone in and pointed her bow at the floor in front of me.

I opened my mouth, not sure what I would say about the dead woman on the floor under Pete's paralyzed form. I knew for sure she was dead, too. I could smell it, and the only heartbeat I could hear was Irina's.

"Freeze!" I looked up at the newcomer. He didn't have a pulse, either.

"Detective Klein, hi." I murmured, running one hand down my face.

"This isn't what I expected to find when I came to congratulate you on that performance." He slapped cuffs on Dave, then sniffed the air. "That's weird." He blinked, then looked down at Pete.

Instead of cuffing the drummer or checking the stake to make sure it hadn't gone all the way through, Klein pushed my paralyzed friend out of the way. He leaned down and inhaled through his nose again. He opened his mouth and licked one of his fangs, which looked about as long as mine felt.

"Hmm." Klein tapped his left ear, and I heard his partner's tinny voice respond. "Backup. Now."

Detective Weaver appeared so fast I would have thought she'd teleported if I hadn't smelled the air of her passage. She'd come through the same way Klein had, just quicker than my eyes could track without enhancement.

"What is it?" Weaver glanced at each of us. I understood why she looked more peeved than usual since all of us were incapacitated. Then she looked at Klein.

"Subdue me." Klein's fists clenched, and he stood entirely too still. "Now."

Weaver didn't bother with cuffs. The stake sprouted instanta-neously from Klein's chest. Whatever Weaver was, her insane speed freaked me out to the extreme.

"You're all coming with me to the PD." Weaver eyed Irina. "Even you, Kazynski."

CHAPTER ELEVEN

Gatto Go

"I told you already, we were onstage." I sighed.

"Time of death is still unconfirmed." Detective Weaver's narrowed eyes shot the attitude equivalent of death rays at me. She was no moon. "You and everyone else on that stage is still on the hook."

"Even Irina?" I raised an eyebrow. She nodded. "You can't be freaking serious."

"I am." Her face barely moved when she spoke. "Just ask Klein. He'll tell you my attitude's more serious than my venom. I turn into a spider, you know."

I gulped, even though vampires don't have to do that kind of thing. I had no idea whether Weaver was the poisonous kind of spider shifter or just bluffing. It'd probably be safer to fight lion-shifting Gatto guys than her. I closed my eyes, thinking about how I'd gone right from the frying pan into the fire.

"Yes, you have." The dry chuckle that followed Weaver's statement meant I'd clichéd aloud. That was the opposite of freaking awesome.

"But how could you guys even suspect Irina?" I tried to put my head in my hands, but the chains between the cuffs and the table didn't reach. I turned my head and scratched the back of my head instead. It wasn't itchy, just an old nervous habit. "That lady was definitely a vampire victim. I could smell it."

"It's related to another case where alive-for-real accomplices were involved." I looked down, listening to Weaver's shoes tap across the stained linoleum as she approached me. I didn't want to look up at her.

"Really? Would you mind telling me about it?" I figured information like that might help Tinfoil Hat fix this mix-up, but even if Weaver said something, how would I get it back to any of my friends?

"I'm not answering any more of your questions." I felt a slight shift in the air and heard a rustle of fabric behind me. "There." When Weaver came back around to the front of the table, she held an evidence bag that looked empty. I knew it wasn't before she sealed it up, though. I could smell what she'd put inside.

"My hair?" I blinked. "I didn't give you permission to take samples."

"I know." She looked down her nose at me. I realized I'd have felt much more comfortable if she smirked like a normal person, but then again, she was the bad cop to Klein's good one. Smirking on the job was probably a no-no as far as she was concerned. "This hair was on our floor."

"Well then, how can you be sure it's mine?" Hope rose in my chest. "Isn't there some kind of law against using compromised evidence?"

"You're the only vampire in Newport with green hair." Weaver paused at the door, her free hand hovering over the knob. "Also, I had the janitor scrub this room thoroughly enough for a surgeon to do organ transplants in here." She opened the door. "See you later, Meyer."

I stared at the scarred tabletop, sure we'd lose the Battle of the

Bands now. But that was what the Gattos wanted at this point. The Mafia shifter boss needed the underdog to win, but after our performance earlier, that was Jack's band, not mine. The wheel of fortune sure liked to run me over.

The door opened again. I didn't want to look up and see Detective Weaver's Gloaty McGloatface. Something jingled nearby, and I would have fallen on the floor if I hadn't been cuffed to the table when a room-temperature hand settled on my shoulder.

"Chill out, Meyer, or I won't be able to unlock these." Detective Klein made good on his words as soon as I stopped freaking out.

"What happened?" I rubbed my wrists even though I didn't have to. "Weaver was all gung-ho about getting a hair sample."

"Yeah, she really loves this job." Klein fluffed the party section of his mullet. "But we got some new information, so you're free to go."

"What about the rest of Night Creatures? Irina Kazynski?" I stood up.

"Yeah, we're releasing them, too."

"Do you mind if I ask why?"

"Nope, I don't mind you asking." He smiled, fangs and all. "Doesn't mean I'm gonna answer, though." Klein dropped a wink. I laughed.

"You could have been on a sitcom, you know that?" I headed out the door he opened for me.

"Yeah, I get that a lot." Klein chuckled. "The only thing people say more is that I should be in one of those detective books."

"Well, why not write one?"

"Nah. I'm no author." The detective responded. "Maybe I should collar one just to see if they would publish a book about me." He elbowed me in the ribs. "Just kidding."

"Yeah, I kinda figured." I did a double-take in the hall as I watched Bianca Brighton head past with a tray of coffee. Now I understood why we'd all gotten released. "She working here or something?"

"Yeah, or something." Klein shrugged. "Trying to get an in for some kind of internship, but we've already got a Tanuki in the technical CSI department this fall. We haven't had a medium since Delilah Redford volunteered on a case in 2001. We're not sure what to do with them, so we're writing Bianca a recommendation to Providence PD." Klein glanced at me. "Hey, isn't she a classmate of yours?"

"Yeah, she is." I nodded. "Hard worker, always helping people without caring whether they're alive, dead, or none of the above."

"Sounds like you should write her a letter, too."

"Maybe I will, but I'm just a student like her."

"Nah." Klein snorted out a laugh. "You're a rock star. Did you know kids in Newport have your posters all over their rooms? My own daughter would have loved you guys even though she's —she would be older than you."

"Really?" I was more surprised about the posters that Klein had a daughter. Vampire kids were hard to come by, and only ever got conceived between a destined vampire couple. I wondered who the mother was, especially since I'd never seen Detective Klein wearing a wedding ring. I hadn't heard of a destined pair who wasn't hitched. Maybe he just didn't wear the ring at work.

"Yeah. You and your band are going places, Lane." Klein smirked. "Someday, I'll get good money for the story of how I arrested your guitarist. And the rest of you, too."

Everyone else was already out in the lobby. I sat down because none of them stood up.

"What are we waiting for?" I fidgeted. "We have to practice our originals for tomorrow night."

"Blaine." Irina leaned back, her violin case resting across her lap. "He's picking us up before Margot gets here. She's lending a Spite to the police investigation."

"Holy moly, a Spite?" I blinked. "Spites are some seriously scary business."

"Well, thanks to the dragon man, you guys don't have to stick around to meet them." Irina rolled her eyes. "I've already met Margot's, though. I wouldn't mind seeing Daryl again and saying hi."

"Daryl?" Pete scratched his head.

"Irina learned the name of Margot's Spite when they helped her and Fred in the Under." I could have sworn Pete had heard the story, but if so, he sure hadn't paid attention.

"Oh." He peered at Irina. "And you remembered? You're a weirdo."

"Yup." She smiled back. We all laughed.

"So, does anyone know how we got released?"

"Yeah." Matt had just walked back through the door. I studied his appearance, because something was different, off, since I'd last seen him before the arrest. He looked unharmed, but the fresh rips and tears in his clothes told me he'd been in yet another unexplained fight and had already healed the wounds.

"Okay, so tell us already," grumbled Pete. Dave nodded his agreement, then pushed his glasses up his nose.

"That medium chick, Bianca? She talked to the dead woman's ghost." Matt leaned against the wall next to a missing person poster of a ten-year-old girl. Something about her face looked awfully familiar, but I couldn't place it. "A vampire killed her, but she didn't fit the description of anyone in either band."

"Wait, *she*?" I blinked. "The mysterious biter is a woman?"

"Yeah, or at least the biter who killed this woman is." Matt twirled one of his dreadlocks. "She was left-handed, but the vampire who bit the blood-loss victim was right-handed."

"Tiamat's scales!" I looked up to see Blaine in the doorway. He tapped the tablet in his hand. "LORA, did you get that?"

"Data accepted," the voice from his device said. "Calculating."

"Okay, let's see what she comes up with." Blaine puffed out a couple of smoke rings.

"No matches found."

"What does that mean, LORA?" I felt weird asking a computer, but I just had to know.

"No registered vampires on Newport this evening are left-handed," LORA stated. "Conclusion, murder perpetrated by an unregistered vampire."

"Stop upstaging me, infernal machine!" Blaine pressed the sync switch and tucked the tablet away in a satchel. "That info's going straight to Kimiko." He jerked his chin at the hall. "She's in there, working. Anyway, I'm here to take you guys back to the hotel before it gets all crispy critters with a chance of Spite out there."

We all waited while Blaine sent LORA's update to Kimiko's phone. An unregistered left-handed vampire? Unregistered vamps were nearly nonexistent. Unless someone had recently unearthed a sleeping one from twenty or more years ago, this one had to be illegally turned. But who would do something like that?

A chill went down my spine as I remembered that Rick the Extramagus supposedly had Mind magic. He'd allegedly used it on the Summoning Professor during the winter, sending creatures to assassinate Henry Baxter. But mind magic only worked on people in a weakened mental state. That meant drugs, which didn't affect vampires or some kind of blood deprivation.

I glanced at everyone, remembering how we'd all rushed that bell-hop in the hall. We'd been drinking bagged blood, though. The hotel provided it as part of the accommodations. No vampire staying there should be hungry enough to accidentally turn someone.

I remembered that first night and seeing Jack go get ice in the middle of his night with Della. We didn't use ice for anything. But a human might. A human bitten enough times in a row might want some ice to take down the swelling. And then there was Nixie's story. Jack had definitely been getting that kind of freaky with Della, and it would leave her vulnerable.

We all piled into the car in front of Newport PD. Something was still bothering me, but not about the hunger or the potential new illegal vampire. No, it was the familiar face on the missing person poster in the police station lobby. I knew that little girl with the bland expression but had no idea where from. I didn't hang out with kids. Even when I was that age, I'd gravitated toward children a couple of years older than me.

I tried thinking about it, but the connection just wouldn't come. Irina went to a quieter room to sleep while the rest of us set up for practice. Maybe music would get my mind in the right state to figure the detail out.

But it didn't come to me until after the Battle of the Bands ended.

CHAPTER TWELVE

Come Original

We'd practiced most of the day, taking turns with the shower beforehand. None of us liked smelling like the Newport jail, even though it was nicer than the Providence one, according to Matt. I didn't even want to know how he knew something like that. Well, actually, I did. I just didn't want to ask in the middle of all that pressure. Something about his disappearances and apparent fights had me curious in a wincing sort of way, and I didn't think either of us had the mental or emotional energy to deal with that conversation.

Irina wouldn't join us on the final night. She'd been awesome to perform with, but she was flat exhausted. I also didn't want her backstage at any point if that hungry left-handed vampire showed up again. Matt, because he hadn't gotten the chance to play with her, tried to argue about it. I put my foot down. He thought no one would be stupid enough to go back there after murdering someone. But he'd never been one to dwell on the early days after we'd been turned.

It sucked, literally and figuratively. Even people who'd

prepared to get turned for years didn't fully understand the hunger they'd have to deal with for eternity. It felt like having a hole in the gut, cold and hollow, where there was supposed to be fullness and warmth. On top of all that, a vampire's nose picked up the scent of blood, living blood, so easily. We'd gone back to the club where we'd been turned over and over, even though it was dangerous to be around that many living people.

Imagine a plate of your favorite food. Now, imagine if you'd been starving for a week. What would you do in that situation if that dish appeared in front of you just then? You'd start stuffing your face until that plate looked like it just came out of a dishwasher. And that's why dead bodies followed the newly turned like flies follow garbage trucks. The deaths were almost always unintentional, but death was final. I refused to risk Irina or any of our other mortal friends that way.

Even worse than vampire stranger danger was the probable half-ton Mafia cat catastrophe. The Gatto Gang didn't discriminate between living and undead. If they had it in for you, that was it. I took a walk up and down the halls, calling Tony to see what he might have to say about that particular issue. The phone went directly to voicemail. Texts went unanswered.

I realized it didn't matter one way or the other. I didn't care anymore what the Gatto guys wanted, half-ton lion shifters or no. Night Creatures was in the Battle of the Bands, finally. We weren't quitting just because some bookies picked different odds to run with. We'd play the final night and let the judges decide. Paul and John didn't seem savvy enough to bribe the folks scoring our performances, so it'd be as fair a contest as possible.

And then, there was Rick the Extramagus. He was the reason for all the monkey-wrenches, the ghosts in our collective machine. But if we got through his tampering, he couldn't mess with us directly anymore. The idea of him indirectly messing with us or hurting our friends sucked, but that hadn't seemed to give the Tinfoil Hatters too much trouble. Then again, people like Lynn, Blaine, and Irina made anything look easy. I felt like Atlas, trying to shrug off my impending impostor syndrome. The others had managed to shoulder the world and pass it along. But I wasn't them. All I could do was my best.

Once we'd practiced as much as we could stand to, we took a short break before getting ready to head to the bandstand. That was when Henrietta Thurston called me. The headmistress of Providence Paranormal College was the last person I expected to hear from unless I'd flunked out of school.

"I want to congratulate you, Mr. Meyer," she said.

"We still have one more set to play before the judges decide, Headmistress."

"I know. I'm not congratulating you for winning." The noise she made was more of a cough than a chuckle.

"Okay, then." I shrugged even though she couldn't see it. "Then what did I do?"

"You made it this far, Lane." Her voice sounded slightly wheezy. I remember thinking that was odd since she'd been recovering from a magical attack, not pneumonia or whatever. Then again, an awful lot of people got sicker from being in the hospital. "If you can handle this, you can make it two more years to graduation."

"Thanks for the vote of confidence, Headmistress." I kept it formal. That made it easier to keep from choking up like a wuss.

"You earned it. Give the rest of Night Creatures my regards."

"I will." She hung up just before the alarm on my phone went off, signaling that it was time to go.

The third night felt much more like an actual battle. Both bands shared the stage, us on the left and them on the right. Jack looked rough around the edges, like he'd been under at least as much stress as I had. I wondered what was wrong, then remembered I hadn't seen Della backstage. Come to think of it, I hadn't scented her around the hotel either. Could they have broken up already?

But no. I couldn't imagine Jack Steele letting anyone dump him. I wondered whether Della was down at the good old Newport PD. I tried imagining her with Weaver and Klein. Something didn't add up when I pictured her face. Then, it computed like LORA on steroids.

I thought back to that poster with the face that had bothered me so much, realizing it was over ten years old. The missing little girl was Della. Della Dawn, who smelled particularly good to vampires for some mysterious reason but even better lately. Where could she have been from age ten to age twenty-something? Human trafficking had been rampant back then. The especially appealing people got turned into dolls, time with them illegally sold to old vamps who longed for something besides bagged blood.

Could Della have been one? She definitely smelled good enough. That would have meant years of being bled, then fed just enough vampire blood to recover for the next shady buyer. I stood there, blinking behind the black curtain, almost forgetting why I was there and that an audience waited on the other side.

"Lane, what's wrong?" Margot's hand waved in front of my face. "It's almost time for curtain up, and you're out to lunch."

"I...It's the new vampire. The one who killed that woman. I think I know who it is." In my mind's eye, I saw Della break up with me, her left hand holding her untouched coffee over the trash can. She was a southpaw.

"Oh, no!" Margot put her hands to her cheeks. "Tell me so I can pass it along to— Crap."

It was too late; the curtain rose. Margot trotted offstage as fast as she could in heels that high. We just stood there, waiting. The Jack Steele Band went first, because we led them by two points, making them the challengers for the evening. I'd have been ecstatic if it weren't for the mystery on my mind and the gazes of the Gattos in the front row. Paul and John smirked at us, and I already knew what they could do. We wouldn't have any "unfortunate accidents" on stage, but afterward, who knew?

Our rivals did a song about the moon; how it took the place of the sun when you're a vampire, how all the changes were beautiful. The sappy lyrics had me incensed. How could Jack, knowing what unlife had been like before the Reveal and after, still play something that out of touch? I had to counter with something that'd drive home the fact that we knew more than those dinosaurs.

I went to each of the guys, telling them my plan. We'd open with the ideological opposite of romanticizing vampirism. Finally, it was our turn. I half-crooned a count of three into the microphone, then strummed chords under Matt's jangling intro. I went through the entirety of *Points* in a state of full immersion.

"Without a doubt, I knew it sucked that night
We'll never win, 'cause no one thinks we're right
We had to walk away, and give up all our plans
Why do I stop and turn around?
And every time I smile they walk away from me
A loser just because I'm fanged, you see
And I'm seen as a guy with blood-lust rage
Why am I stuck on this page?
Eternity spent in a cage
What's the point again?
What's the point again?
And every night, I know I'm not alone
Needing a glove to use a smartphone
I have to deal with cops
Just throwing us in jail
Suspected for my fangs, you see
And every time I smile they walk away from me

A loser just because I'm fanged, you see
And I'm still trying just to find what's mine
Why do people think it's fine?
Eternity spent in a cage
What's the point again?
What's the point again?
And every time I smile they walk away from me
A loser just because I'm fanged, you see
At forty-five I look like twenty-three
Why do you look down on me?
Eternity spent in a cage
What's the point again?
What's the point again?
Spending all my money on the blood bank fees
Like we're mosquitoes maybe even fleas
The blood suppliers love that bottom line
Are we just a new economy?
Eternity spent in a cage
What's the point again?
What's the point again?"

I couldn't be sure, but the crowd seemed to cheer louder for us than they had for the Jack Steele Band. Our rivals were the better musicians in a technical sense, but events over the past month, especially the last few days, had Night Creatures buzzing with a raw emotion the other group just couldn't match, especially when it came to the cold, hard facts of being undead.

We waited through another of Jack's originals. I immediately recognized it as something he'd written and polished while I'd been his student. It was all about grief and outliving mortal loved ones. Still a sappy, sentimental song, though. I knew exactly which one of ours would kick its ass.

Jack's song was about lying down and letting grief roll over you. Ours was all about fighting back because I'd written it right after Dad's diagnosis. I didn't think they'd find a cure for Alzheimer's before his time was up, but I knew damn well I wasn't giving up on him because of it. I'd made a promise and stuck to it, and him. And that was what our second song was all about.

"This one's for you, Dad," I said over Dave's bass intro. Cheering started in the Tinfoil Hat section and cascaded across the crowd. I wondered how they knew about my father. Had Margot told them? It didn't matter. I sang in defiance of Dr. Alois Alzheimer and his damn disease.

"So your mind is falling to pieces
Memory just temp like leases
You need family, help with your head
Older, stronger, but not wiser
I'm there when your mind plays miser
No more rote, you time warp instead
I can't predict your mind or headspace
Even if you don't remember my face
I promise to be there for you
Even nights, you ask, "Who are you?"
I'll never give up because it's true
Your mind's changed but your heart's the same."

I bopped all over the stage during Matt's guitar solo and Pete's drum-fest, pumping my fist in the air, because *Dementia* was a freaking anthem, not a ballad. When we came back around to repeat the chorus, I snagged the mic from its stand and continued my trajectory. At the center of our section of the stage, I squatted and leaned forward, directing my defiant attitude at the Gatto goons in the front row. They might not be a mind-stealing disease, but they'd do as targets to rail against.

The Gattos had to know we were just going to do our thing and damn their threats and consequences. Now, they understood that we wouldn't take that bucket of crap lying down. Punks like us never did, not from big-cat Mafiosos or horrible mind-sucking diseases.

The crowd definitely loved us more after song number two. As I set the mic back in the stand, I caught Jack looking at me. His grim grin also came with a short nod. He saw how things were going. If we countered him like this again, we'd win the whole shebang, and my old mentor knew it. It was weird, noticing his distinct lack of hostility, which made no sense to me at that point. It was like some morbid viral video of watching someone smile for the camera just before tumbling headlong into the Grand Canyon.

Jack's third song almost felt like he'd conceded and passed us a torch. I wondered why he'd picked another ballad to do, then it dawned on me. He'd decided to play what he loved this time. He didn't care anymore what was popular or what would win. Like Olivia had said back on the first night, Jack wasn't hungry. All the guy wanted was to do what he loved. I realized then that all of The Jack Steele Band's popularity, all their acclaim, had been a necessary evil to Jack. He'd had to adjust to the Reveal and help all of us by blazing a trail, making a case through music that vampires weren't always villains.

That was why our third song felt so bittersweet. I knew we'd be blowing them away and taking up the mantle of champions. I hadn't expected Jack to treat me like an equal instead of his student in this final contest. He moved on as we moved up, determined to surpass what had come before. I wondered whether the crowd had any idea. I knew that at least one person out there did: Irina. She stood there, holding up a phone as she recorded the whole thing, probably so she could take it to the Under and show Fred. A pang hit my heart; I wished my best friend could be here.

"What's this unlife without you around?
Oh, I don't really live, now.
Should be in the ground.
I try existing like I did before,
Need permission to walk in your door,
And I ask, where's my crazy life?
Can't drink beer or wine, don't taste alive no more,
And you won't see me anymore,
Since I turned,
But the life I want still has you in it,
I'll have to find one with a moonlit view,
And I'm haunting all the places that we used to,
I hold those days so tightly, ones I spent with you,
I wait hoping you'll come around,
But I should be in the ground."

As the last note of *Grounded* faded, the crowd was nearly silent. I worried for half a moment, but then sound erupted, volcanic cheering. I closed my eyes, trying to imagine a warm summer downpour in place of the sound, but the image that conjured itself instead was an embrace like an autumn blanket. It was the sort of applause that begged for an encore. Too bad that was against the contest rules.

Pete, Dave, and Matt stepped up beside me. We stood in a line, shoulder to shoulder like undead soldiers of rock. When the judges made their announcement, we all hung our heads at first. It wasn't until Jack clapped me on the shoulder as he headed offstage that I understood. We'd won.

I stared out at the crowd, unblinking, mouth open. The moment before the lights went down, I noticed the empty space where the Gattos had been. I dashed offstage, tumbling over Jack at the foot of the steps.

"*Oof!*" I had a face full of dirt but saw the reason Jack had stopped anyway. "Oh, no. No way."

"Do you know whose bag this is?" Jack pointed at the over-turned green handbag.

"Margot Malone's." I closed my eyes.

"The Summoner reporter?" Jack's voice wavered.

"Yeah." I opened my eyes again. I wouldn't just give up or turn this over to the police, but I had too many suspicions and not enough information. I looked, really looked this time. "That poster." I pointed at the glossy eight by ten print I'd last seen in the Newport PD lobby. "You saw it before, Jack?"

"No, but I know who it's a picture of." He shuddered. I waited, wondering whether his answer would match my guess. "Della."

I had no idea what that shudder was about, so I looked at Jack's face to find his eyes misty with tears. I caught a whiff of something familiar on the poster in his hand and understood everything. It all fell into place. Well, all but one piece about my ex-girlfriend did, anyway.

"You're destined." I stood up and dusted myself off. "You and Della."

"Lane—"

"You've known it for years, too." I shook my head, cutting him off before he could get another sound out. "That was why you tossed that magic lure perfume she had." His mouth dropped open. "Yeah, I always knew she used it. Della didn't need that stuff to pull you in, though, and you didn't want competition. But you didn't think the hotel staff would actually use it."

"Okay, you figured it out." Jack hung his head even lower. "I'm sorry you got blamed for that poor woman last night since it was actually her."

"So, Della is a vampire." I narrowed my eyes. "Did you turn her?"

"No." Jack peered at me, clearly puzzled. He must have wondered how much I knew. "I'm crazy in love, not just plain crazy." Jack closed his eyes, one of those lone manly tears trickling down his cheek.

"How'd it happen, then?"

"I don't know." He sighed. "But all that perfume, a hotel full of vampires. One of them must have drained her by accident."

"That doesn't make sense." I sat up, gathering Margot's scattered things and stuffing them back in her bag. I decided to play dumb. "Unless someone gave her their blood before."

"But they did." He held up the poster, then dropped it. "Where do you think she was for ten years?"

"Oh, boy." I watched the card stock see-saw its way through the air to land on the ground. "So she really was a doll."

"Yup, kept for the old-schoolers who think the new laws are guidelines." Jack closed his eyes.

"Old-schoolers like you." I narrowed my eyes and bared my fangs, prepared as much as I could for a fight I probably wouldn't win.

"No." Jack let out a long breath. "It wasn't like that. I owed the police a favor. I helped them uncover the place they had her and a bunch of other kids in. When I saw her, I knew, but she was so young and so weak. I waited, maybe too long. I'm sorry about how we got together, right after you two dated and all."

"It's okay, Jack. I understand about you and Della. Destiny happens." I noticed what looked like an amber marble next to Jack's foot. "Where are they, then?"

CHAPTER THIRTEEN

Dawn with the Sickness

"I don't know where she is, Lane." He shrugged. "But look at that." Jack pointed at a bare patch of ground. I saw the imprint of Della's boots, Margot's pumps, and what looked like wingtips. No one I knew wore those, but they seemed like stereotypical mobster shoes.

"Okay, three sets of footprints."

"And they don't go anywhere." Jack clenched his hands into fists. "If they did, you sure as hell wouldn't have tripped over me."

"I think I have a solution to that problem. Margot's a Summoner, and these are her friends' anchors. Two years at PPC have taught me that much, at least." I grabbed the marble and closed my hand around it. "Margot needs help," I said to no one in particular.

I saw probably the last thing I wanted to right then—a Spite. The Seelie hunting hounds were warped and twisted creatures. When the Sidhe Queen wanted to punish a Sprite, she shredded their wings and turned them into a Spite. They could track anything, were virtually tireless, and ate magic.

This one had to be Daryl, the Spite Irina and Fred had borrowed in the Under. They looked me in the eye, then sniffed around the room, paying particular attention to the footprints. They whined, then pointed just like a normal hunting dog might. I nodded at them and stood up. Jack got off the stairs, finally letting the rest of Night Creatures pass.

"We'd better go with you." Matt stepped up next to me. Pete and Dave nodded their agreement.

"No way." I shook my head. "That Extramagus is still around. Find the rest of our friends and stay safe. I think three vampires, a Summoner, and a Spite can handle a couple of big-cat shifters."

"The Gatto Gang?" Jack bared his teeth. "You think they're behind this?"

"Well, they've been harassing us the whole time since we got into this contest, so they must be. Wanna rescue your girl?" I smirked at Jack. "Follow that hound!" I took off after Daryl with my old mentor on my heels.

We followed the Spite toward the Fort Adams Redoubt. The night was humid and sultry, with air that almost felt too heavy for the sea breezes to lift. The faerie hound didn't run up to the entrance. Instead, they made a sharp left, baying as they took off across an athletic field toward Sail Newport on Brenton Cove.

Daryl's feet clicked on the wood our feet thudded on. At the end, a rowboat was waiting. The Spite leaped in, and I went with them cautiously. Jack just stood there, staring at the water.

"Come on, already." I beckoned him over with one hand, the other rummaging in Margot's bag for the anchor I hoped was still in it.

"This is theft." Jack pointed at the boat.

"I don't care." My fingers snagged something woody and weathered. Driftwood? A water faerie then, one I knew. I pulled it out and conjured up the memory of clothes made from fish scales.

Jack sighed, shaking his head as though it weighed a ton.

Before he could say more, I heard someone clearing their throat behind me. I turned and saw exactly the familiar face I'd hoped for.

"Nixie!" I smiled at Margot's other pure faerie friend.

"Hi, Lane." They looked up at Jack. "We're not stealing this boat, Mr. Steele." Nixie giggled.

"What? " Jack scratched his head.

"Check it out." Nixie pointed at the name on whatever nautically inclined people call the back end of a boat.

"*The Dragon Man*," Jack read.

"It's Blaine Harcourt's boat!" I waved my arms, more like I was drowning than sitting in a seaworthy craft. "We're friends. If there's a problem, he'll say he let us use it. Get in, already!"

Jack got in and sat in the center of the boat with his hands folded, looking like a model for the directive "keep your arms and legs inside the ride at all times" that always got tossed around at amusement parks. I wondered for a moment whether he was afraid of the ocean or something, but then Nixie clapped their hands and the boat started moving. Jack shuddered. Maybe he was hydrophobic.

I wasn't sure where the boat headed, exactly, not even with my vampiric ability to see better in the dark than regular folks. The salt air drowned out just about every other scent, too. That didn't seem to be a problem for Daryl. The Spite stood in the front of the boat, pointing with their nose while Nixie made course corrections every time the queen's hound turned. I thought about all the nearest land masses and hoped it wouldn't take long. It didn't. And Daryl didn't lead us to land.

We sat, looking up at a yacht. It wasn't too big as far as luxurious boats went. Actually, I didn't know diddly squat about that. I just knew the boat was not much more than twice as big as the one we rode in, but looked ten times more luxurious. That was a feat and a half, considering the Harcourts were billionaire dragons.

"How do we get on?" I looked around for a rope or a ladder, but there wasn't one.

"We stop thinking like humans and do this." I felt a shift in equilibrium as Jack leaped straight up, landing on the other deck.

"Showoff," I mumbled, then imitated him.

Jack caught me before I vaulted over the big, glass-encased area behind him. I hadn't realized that leaping up from a boat on the water would be so springy. I grinned at my old teacher. Actually, it was more like a wince. He just shook his head and pointed. I turned and saw Daryl had followed us. The Spite led the way, pacing toward a door. We followed.

When we pulled it open, we saw steps. Jack cocked his head, listening. I heard nothing, but he nodded, so I figured he must have enhanced his hearing a little. I hadn't, because I wanted to save all my energy for the inevitable fight or flight from the two Gatto goons I expected.

At the bottom of the stairs, I froze. Jack did no such thing, of course. The man in yellow who stood behind the ladies bound in back-to-back chairs was nothing to him. The figure looked dandified, not intimidating to a stranger like Jack, but I knew this asshole. I had been burned by him before. Literally. And that was no shifter.

"Richard Hopewell." I smiled, baring my fangs. "I've heard so many sucky things about you, it feels as if I know you."

"And you are?" The middle-aged Extramagus looked down his nose at me, tilting the brim of his round hat up slightly.

"Hi, I'm Lane Meyer." I rummaged in Margot's bag again, hoping to find her friend the imp's anchor. We could have used a miracle right then. I kept up the hopefully distracting chatter but found nothing. "No one ever formally introduced us, but I don't give a rat's ass about formalities. I'm a punk, and proud of it."

"Lane—" Jack tugged my sleeve, stopping my angry forward trajectory. I glanced at him, then followed his gaze.

My shin had almost made contact with a trip-wire. I

narrowed my eyes and stepped over it. Jack and Daryl followed, the latter directing a faint whine in Margot's direction. She looked at me, puzzled. I wondered why.

"So, the punk rocker's been hiding his real talent."

"What the hell does that mean?" As soon as the question was out of my mouth, I realized it was redundant. I blinked. Sure, I'd used Margot's anchors, but those were only supposed to work for Summoners. They weren't like the one-time-use Psychic papers she'd given Fred in the Under. I had been the one summoning Daryl and then Nixie. I wasn't just a regular vampire, after all. I'd had a Psychic ability all along, one of the hardest to master, and most often overlooked. Most people didn't encounter pure faerie creatures for long enough to discover a bond with them. I'd been most people before getting turned.

"Ah, I see. You didn't even know it yourself until tonight. Such a shame you bloomed so late." Richard grinned. "But the jazzman is still just as mundane as ever."

"I don't care what kind of catty comments you fire at us, pal." Jack cracked his knuckles and bared his fangs. "Give Della back and I won't drain you dry."

"Um, Jack?" It was my turn to elbow him. "He's an Extramagus. Got literal fire, and who knows what else."

"Oh." Jack cleared his throat. "Still. Let those ladies go, and we won't have any trouble."

"Let them go?" Richard raised an eyebrow. "I can't do a thing like that. One's an unregistered vampire, and the other's got illegal magic perfume on her. I've made a citizen's arrest because unlike you, I'm an upstanding member of society."

"No, you're not." I stood up straight, finding I had about a half-inch on Jack. "I know what you did last semester."

"Personally, I did nothing but mind my own business." Richard's smile looked soft, like velvet covering a set of brass knuckles.

"If that's not a loaded statement, I don't know what is." Della's voice made me blink. Even though her words dripping venom, her face was as placid as a pond. "You're the one who sold me the magic perfume you planted on Margot, and I'll tell anyone who'll listen."

"And there's your problem." Richard's smile had my temper feeling like a nuclear device. "No one will listen, not to an unregistered vampire."

"That doesn't matter." Jack scoffed. "They'll listen to me." He grinned at me. "To us."

"They can't listen to ashes." Richard's words and worse, his sunny smile, had me dashing to the girls in the chairs. "It's such a shame these talented fellows resisted my citizen's arrest."

"No!" I stepped between them and Richard. Jack followed suit without even knowing what was coming. I souped myself up with the energy from the bagged blood back at the hotel, then I picked up both chairs and hurled them toward the only cover, a bar in a corner behind me.

Jack looked confused, but he enhanced himself similarly and headed over, dragging the ladies the rest of the way behind the solid-wood structure. I could only hope the bar would cast enough of a shadow to protect them. I made a break for it, but Richard caught me by the collar.

"You're not going anywhere." The man in yellow grinned, reminding me of the time I'd come across a skull on the beach on Cape Cod after the Boston Internment. "Well, perhaps you'll go in a pretty urn on my mantle. Then again, perhaps not. I never liked you punks and your music."

"Hit me with your best shot, bastard," I spat, gnashing my teeth and swinging my fists the way Jack was swinging at the wall behind the bar if the sound of splintering wood was any indication. My fists couldn't reach Richard, though. He had me in a vise-grip, and some kind of magic shield protected the rest of his body from me. I reached up, making one last-ditch effort to remove the hand he had wound in my hair. No use. I was stuck.

Only one kind of faerie or changeling could use glamour as a force-field, and Richard was it.

I wished I could at least get a message to Tinfoil Hat and tell them what I'd discovered. Richard was definitely a changeling, as they'd thought, but I knew now that he was a Sidhe. I had no idea how that information would help them, but they'd be able to do something with it. At that moment, all I could think of was that this was it.

And that was okay with me. I'd given probably the best stage performance I'd ever have in me. I'd saved three people I cared about, and I'd done the right thing by my family. I closed my eyes, feeling a strange yet welcome peace ripple from me, as though I was the stone dropped in the pond for once instead of the other way around. I knew that Richard killing me here in Narragansett Bay would leave blood on his hands, and I was high-profile enough for it to count. He wouldn't get away with killing Lane freaking Meyer, or not without consequences, anyway.

But I'd forgotten someone. Maybe it was because they were quadrupedal and fierce, but before that night, I'd always thought of Spites as the intellectual equals of dogs. Daryl was sentient, though. They were probably more intelligent than me, and when a pure faerie inserted themself into any equation, imbalance resulted.

In case you don't know, Spites eat magic. When Rick the Dick fired his hands up with his Spectral magic, Daryl ate the spell like a mundane hound snatches food from a kid's hands. When the Extramagus cranked up the power, determined to give me a sunburn, the Spite just opened their mouth and drank it down. All I got was singed.

Richard dropped me, extending both hands to go to town on poor Daryl. I couldn't imagine what kind of magic he'd use, though. The only counter to a Spite was something Seelie, helped along with a little Luck. Or a Null Magus. I remember putting out the last of the smoldering around my neck, thinking about how coursework at PPC had taught me more than I thought I knew.

"Lane! Daryl!" I turned my head to see Margot vaulting over the bar, holding something that looked like a bamboo spear. My conversation with Rick had given Jack enough time to free the ladies, as well as start knocking a hole in the wall. Margot had armed herself with another of her friends, a brownie wearing a pointy bronze helmet. It crackled with what I assumed was rage and then she let it fly, its business end aimed at the attacking Extramagus' head.

Then everything slowed down. It was like when a movie shows some ultra-fast superhero, except it was a big, powerful faerie instead of Quicksilver or the Flash.

"Cease this nonsense." The Sidhe Queen flicked a pinkie in Rick's general direction. The brownie clattered to the floor, and Daryl sat like a good doggie.

"Y-your Majesty." Margot curtsied so deep, I was afraid she'd get swept away in the undertow. She held that pose for the entire conversation, too. Her thighs had to be more incredible than the Hulk's.

"Majesty." Richard bowed, whisking his hat off his head with a flourish.

"Miss Malone." The queen stared at Margot. "Your contract with this Spite is dissolved. You may enter my demesne to find another after three nights' time."

"Thank you, Your Majesty." I wondered why she was thanking the queen instead of arguing for her companion, but then she spoke again. "I invoke my right to knowledge, as my contract permits. What will become of this Spite?"

"It's being called into service by my newest knight." The queen snapped her fingers and Daryl stepped to her side, heeling better than an American Kennel Club champion. I blinked back tears of relief because I knew the queen's newest knight—Fred. Daryl would be in good hands. Margot murmured a second thanks, then some other words which sent the brownie away. That was good since Brownies and water didn't mix.

"Um, excuse me, Your Majesty." I waited for the queen to acknowledge me. "How did you know to come here just in time?" The Sidhe monarch glanced down and waited.

"That was me, Lane." A tiny and familiar voice came from somewhere near the queen's feet.

"Nixie?"

"Yeah, I knew her Glorious Majesty wanted to call Daryl back, so I told her where they were." The Pixie didn't say any more, but they didn't have to. I understood. They knew Rick was on the boat the whole time and waited for the right moment to call in a rescue. There was no way the queen didn't have some idea, either.

"The Spite isn't the only creature I require from this boat." The queen turned her head, gazing at Richard. "You will return to my throne room in two minutes precisely. Finish your business here in that time if you can. I do not tolerate tardiness in a prospective consort, regardless of his personal circumstances."

With those words, the queen, Daryl, and Nixie vanished.

The four of us vampires were alone with an Extramagus wielding Spectral magic and God only knew what else who had one minute to kill us. There was only one thing to do about that.

CHAPTER FOURTEEN

Kiss Me Undeadly

"Jump ship!" I dashed behind the bar, calling all my strength to finish busting open the wall behind it. Shards of glass pinged and clanged to the floor. Margot dove out the window, her yellow dress snagging and bringing the rest of the glass into the brine with her.

"Go!" I elbowed Della, hollering in her ear. She didn't budge, just held onto something on the floor. I looked down and understood the problem immediately. "Follow Margot. I've got Jack."

Della's sob lingered on the ocean breeze as she jumped. I dragged at Jack's arm, maintaining the extra strength, and pulled him up to the window, thinking he was unconscious. He wasn't.

"Leave me." He turned his head to look at Richard. No, that wasn't right. Jack was looking away from what frightened him, not toward.

"Look, the ocean's scary, but I'm sure it doesn't want you today." I pulled him again, harder this time. "Della's out there. Isn't she your destiny or something?"

Jack said nothing, just jerked his chin down once and dove

out the window after the others. And there I was, alone again with Tricky Rick and all his magic, except he was just standing there smirking. I made like a tree and got out of there.

"Come on in, Lane, the water's fine!" My sarcasm got whipped away by the balmy sea breeze, but even summer didn't make the Bay warm. It was like jumping into a pitcher of ice water, except with the stickiness only saltwater had. My head surfaced, and I spluttered around a mouthful of seaweed. "Eww."

I saw *The Dragon Man*, with all three of my waterlogged allies on board. While flailing my arms, one hand bumped something solid. I grabbed it, realizing it was the side of Blaine's boat. I looked up, and let go almost immediately after.

"Die, already!" Rick stood on *The Dragon Lady's* deck and blasted the smaller watercraft with a fireball from the yacht's deck. I heard three splashes, which meant my friends were okay.

Instinct kicked in and I tried to swim away, but the tenacious current wouldn't let me. I floundered, feeling more like a piece of driftwood than a living, thinking person. Rick blasted out three more fireballs over my head, and I craned my neck. The boat looked like a brazier at WaterFire instead of a dinghy or what-ever it had been. Bits of it fell, splashing into the drink. I glared back up at Richard, taking a deep breath to sling the worst cuss words I could think of at him because I had nothing else left.

It was almost as though the Extramagus couldn't see me. He peered across the water, his hand surrounded by fire phasing through red, orange, yellow, and blue. Something grabbed me by the back of my neck. It was warm, five-fingered, and tipped with claws. I struggled, trying to break free.

"Chill out, Lane." I recognized that voice—Matt. I stilled long enough for what or whoever was attached to that hand to haul me on board. "When the Spite poofed out of the police station, they knew there was trouble."

Everyone was there. Well, not exactly. But Dave, Pete, and Matt stood on the deck of a tugboat. Jack and Della huddled under sodden towels. Margot rushed to my side and wrapped a threadbare beach towel around my shoulders. Blaine leaned against a stack of crates, flanked by Bianca and Detective Klein. Kimiko and Olivia hunkered down, peering at the tablet running LORA.

"Once we realized the Gattos weren't the real problem, we came to help." Kimiko looked up, jerking her chin at whoever was behind me. I turned to have a look, my eyes finding a statuesque woman who even more physically intimidating than Nox Phillips. Her ruddy hair was spiky and wild, more like a mane or ruff. Tiny tusks poked from her lower lips like reverse and more visible fangs. Her hands had claws instead of fingernails. All the same, they were painted neon pink. Troll ladies still wanted to feel girly. Who knew?

"You know a troll, Kim?" I blinked at the faerie in question, waiting for an introduction or something.

"Sure do!" Kimiko sounded like having a troll for a friend was the highlight of her night, but she gave me an excellent reason a moment later. "Gemma saved Blaine and me during Spring Break."

"Well, I guess we all owe you one, Gemma. It's good to meet you." I hugged Margot close. After a moment of stiff surprise on her part, she hugged me back. I almost melted, but curiosity kept me together. "I have to ask; how come Rick the Dick can't see us?"

"That's a funny story, actually." The troll smirked. "This is my grandpa's boat. He's got it glamoured like woah. Your dragon friend here figured the bad guy wouldn't want to use any glamour-penetrating faerie magic this close to tithing. And also, we had a little extra help beefing up our invisibility from Detective Klein."

"Detective Weaver's the one you should thank." Klein put his hands on his hips. "She's been working on a spider-shifter-silk device with your Headmistress ever since those vampire murders back in the winter. Even if he'd used faerie magic to see through the glamour, it wouldn't have worked."

"Well, thank her for me, then." I smiled at Detective Klein. He smiled back and gave me a thumbs-up.

"And what about the Gatto debt?"

"Oh, I paid that." Blaine waved his hand.

"Thought you were tapped out?" I raised an eyebrow, suddenly as skeptical about the dragon shifter as he usually was about Tony.

"Yeah, I am when it comes to five-hundred large in bail money." Blaine blew out a smoke ring. "But all they wanted was two grand. That's like two dollars for me."

Everyone else laughed, but I waited, watching as Richard used up the tail end of the queen's two minutes. When his time ended, a glowing portal opened to his left. I heard his teeth grinding in frustration as he stepped through. A breath I'd forgotten about holding let itself out of my lungs as I faced the rest of Night Creatures. I scanned Matt longer than the others. His clothes were all torn up again. No one else's were.

"Matt, I know we've been arguing lately, and I don't want to start again." I looked Matt right in the eye. It was finally time; I couldn't wait anymore. "I have to know why you're always getting in fights and turning up with your clothes destroyed. You've been hiding something so hard, you got yourself arrested. What gives?"

"Man, this is more the kind of conversation people have in private." Matt looked down at his feet. Even his stompy boots were messed up, their soles held together with duct tape.

"I think it's going to come out anyway." Margot untangled herself from my arms and sat up. "I wouldn't go there in any of my pieces, but I've noticed what's been going on with you. I also saw some, um, less reputable reporters catch you in the act."

"Well, I guess you all better hear it from me first." Matt's head hung lower than I thought possible. "I hit on the wrong people.

I'm a wreck because I keep getting into fights when I try flirting with anyone. You guys can replace me if you want to."

"Um, maybe I'm denser than lead or something, but I don't get what you're saying, dude." I got up and walked over to my friend, the best guitarist I'd ever collaborated with, and put my hand on his shoulder. "Just lay it out as plain and simple as you can."

"All right, Lane." Matt managed to look me in the eye, although he trembled. He took a deep breath. "I'm gay."

"Okay." I squeezed his shoulder.

"Okay?" He blinked. Everyone else on the boat nodded, either grinning or smiling. "You mean, none of you have a problem with that?"

"No. Why would we?" I grinned. Murmurs of support and approval sprouted around us like blossoms on the branches of friendship. "You're our friend, Matt. Besides, this is the twenty-first century. We're all out about drinking blood and our sun allergies, so why not this? You be you, man." I clapped him on the shoulder one more time, then dropped my arm.

"Thanks." The smile started in Matt's eyes, and I knew he'd checked our answers with his lie-detecting power. It made sense to me. I'd have done the same thing if I'd been in his shoes. I blinked, not sure whether I was all misty-eyed from the feels or the salt spray on the deck. We'd all grown from these cocka-mamie experiences, and not apart, either. Together.

"Can I quote you guys on that?" Margot stepped up beside me, her pen hovering over a notepad too sodden to write on.

"You can quote me on anything you've heard this weekend." I chuckled. "And whatever I say over coffee tomorrow night, too. That is if you'll agree to go out with me?"

"Anytime, Lane." It was Margot's turn to chuckle. "Anytime." The coolness of her lips as she pressed them to my cheek felt like the intro to the greatest and best song in the world.

CHAPTER FIFTEEN

Better Off Undead

I headed down Thayer Street, nodding at Jack and Della in the window of Blue State Coffee. After that, I went up Camp to get to Hope. I had to meet everyone over at the Dennisons' and wasn't sure what to expect. When I got there, I turned up the driveway, passing what looked like brass gates. I thought that was weird until I remembered Josh and Nox were mates and Ren intended to keep trying to win Beth back. Having the traditional wrought-iron would have put any faeries spending time here in danger.

"Hey." Margot met me at the top of the drive and slipped her hand into mine, then led me along the side of the house to a door. We entered and went down a flight of stairs to find ourselves in a basement rec room. It had a bar, a billiards table, sofas, and a TV with game systems hooked up. Blaine and Kimiko were playing one of those guitar games, and she was kicking his butt. Josh cleared his throat but let them finish their match.

"Okay, so, now's when we fill each other in and give all the data to LORA." Josh gestured at empty seats, glancing at me, Margot, Blaine, and Kimiko. Everyone else was already sitting down. Well, except for Henry and Maddie. They were peering from a laptop on the bar, Skyping from Vermont. Once I sat, Josh spoke again. "Lane, you start."

I told them everything. Most of them already knew most of my version of stuff, although I hadn't intended to reveal my visit to the nursing home with Margot. But something nagged at my memory of that evening. I paused when I talked about Jan and how she'd had an unexpectedly emotional reaction to a bonding experience between two vampires.

"Do you think this Jan lady is a Precognitive Psychic?" Maddie's voice piped tinnily from the laptop's speakers.

"Maybe." I shrugged. "I guess she could be."

"Well, there's no Precog named Jan in the Registry." Olivia tapped a tablet, using her Law Student credentials to access the record. "No Telepaths either, and a woman her age would definitely be in there."

"Wait, her age? How old is she? What's she look like?" That was Henry talking through the computer, this time.

I described Jan. Henry's eyes went wide.

"So, she's familiar to the memory man," Josh smirked. "Gotta love coincidence."

"She's familiar to me, too." Kimiko's voice startled me. "From a very particular blocked memory." She looked at Blaine. "Should be the same for you, dragon man."

"Yeah." Blaine sighed. "We'll have to do our mate mind-meld on this before Henry gets back, but I think you're right. I think this Jan was the Precog presiding over our betrothal."

"Betrothal?" I blinked at Blaine, then Kimiko. Neither answered, although he reached over and brushed her bangs off her forehead. She did the same for him. I saw matching scars, mirror images. "I still don't get it."

"It's how dragon families arrange marriages," Blaine answered me, still gazing into his mate's eyes. "The scar works like one of Henry's memory trinkets. Huh, guess that means there was a

Memory Psychic there, too. Kimi and I are older than we look. Henry would have been way too young back then."

"Hold that thought, Blaine." Josh stood up. "You and Henry talk about this when they get back."

"Okay." Henry nodded on-screen, and Blaine nodded back.

"Bianca, give us your report. Well, you and Pete." Josh nodded at my drummer, who'd tucked himself in the corner by the fridge.

"After Nox had to beat you guys up in the hall and LORA came up with that coincidence, I knew something extra-weird was going on." Bianca leaned against the bar instead of the back of her stool, cocking her head to the right. She nodded, and I figured Horace was there with her. "Once you guys agreed to let me help find out who turned you, I asked Pete to investigate some stuff at the hotel while I went to the hospital and the PD. Take it away, Pete."

"Yeah, so, I found out there was a bagged-blood theft from the hotel's stores." He shook his head. "Made no sense since that comes with sunless rooms, so I knew there had to be some other vamp around who wasn't staying with us."

"Hold on. Wasn't Della an unregistered vampire?" Lynn had her hand up like Hermione Granger in Snape's potions class.

"I'm getting to that." Pete scratched his goatee. "This is more about how she got to be that way. Anyhow, we think the blood thief was also responsible for the blood-loss victim Matt and Jack got arrested for."

"Yeah, makes sense." I hadn't even noticed that Tony was there with us. He'd stuck to the shadows behind the bar, probably to stay out of Blaine's way. "Go on, drummer boy."

"Nah, it's Bianca's turn." Pete nodded at her. "She's the one who talked to the chick."

"Okay, so, I went to the hospital and interviewed the lady's ghost. She said a guy with a big purple Mohawk bit her." Bianca turned to Pete again.

"Do you remember that guy, Lane?" Pete shuddered.

"Yeah. Used to bounce most of the venues we played back before we got turned." I raised an eyebrow. "Never knew he was a vampire, probably because bouncers never smile."

"Well, he was. Is." Pete shook his head again. "Anyway, Bianca and Horace think he drained Della but didn't know she'd turn because she used to be a doll."

"That's right." Bianca nodded. "We think he got paid to do it, too." She tilted her head. "Both that victim and Della told us their attacker had brand-new boots and a leather jacket. Those are pretty expensive. We think Purple Mohawk was trying to sabotage the Battle of the Bands by attacking Della after the odds turned toward the Night Creatures. She mentioned he said Mr. Gitano sent his regards."

"Not this Mr. Gitano, either." Tony's eyes narrowed, but not before I noticed them go catlike. "My dad's pawprints are all over this. I think he's been dealing with Rick the Dick since Spring Break. The Reveal wasn't good for his business, and if Richard's been trying to buck those changes, it makes sense for dear old Dad to get a piece of that action."

"So, what are you going to do about it?" Blaine sneered around the question, glaring at Tony through the smoke around his head. The cat shifter rolled his eyes, lip curling in preparation for some kind of scathing response, but their pack Alpha butted in.

"Well, the police are looking for Mr. Purple Mohawk now." Josh's smile reminded me of a graveyard under a full moon. "APB statewide, one of two."

"So, that was how Della got off the hook." Margot nodded gravely. "They're holding that guy responsible for the poor woman backstage as well as her attempted murder and illegal turn. I wonder whether he had anything to do with you guys being turned?"

"Maybe." I sighed. "If they catch him, we'll know."

"We could find out sooner." Bianca tilted her head, listening.

"Horace just reminded me that we can get in to see Professor Watkins tomorrow. After that, it's just a matter of following his silver thread to track him down and question him."

"How's this going to help with the Extramagus?" I wasn't sure what Bianca meant by the silver thread but figured it was some Psychic medium thing.

"Well, Detective Klein being on Gemma's boat and actually seeing Richard Hopewell shoot a fireball at Lane and company is huge." Josh grinned like a wolf in the henhouse.

"Gemma?" Sir Albert Dunstable stood from his chair, where he'd been taking notes silently. "Gemma Tolland?" The Sidhe's lips were parted, his cheeks flushed, and his heart rate up. I'd never imagined he could lose his composure like that. "The troll changeling?"

"Well, she's tithed to the king, but yeah." I shrugged, glad I knew a thing or two about faeries. "Gemma's the one who fished us out of the drink. You know her?"

"Not since before I tithed." Al sat back down heavily, his expression distant and wistful.

I wondered what kind of history a Seelie Sidhe knight and an Unseelie troll could possibly have. I would have suggested he give her a call sometime, but I knew nothing could happen between faeries pledged to different courts. Poor Al. I glanced around the room. The empathy was almost palpable, and I knew that, in the future, Tinfoil Hat would have the knight's back the same way they'd had mine.

"Anyway..." Josh broke the silence to continue the matter at hand. "Richard made a big mistake by using the one school of magic he's registered under. The remains of Blaine's boat have his recorded energy signature all over it, and that's who the second APB is for."

"No arrest warrant out for Mr. Gitano?" Blaine still glared at Tony. Kimiko slipped her arm around his waist.

"Once we have enough evidence, there will be. We'll get more during Professor Brodsky's trial in the fall." Olivia shuffled over to the bar and sat next to Bianca, putting herself between the angry dragon and the cat shifter. "I'm working on that with Mr. Ichiro, so get on my case if it's too slow."

"Fine." Blaine turned back toward the TV, picking up the guitar-shaped controller. He cycled through songs as the rest of us breathed a sigh of relief. The last thing anyone wanted was Blaine losing his temper at Tony and going all fiery on us.

"Knowing all this stuff is nice, but it all still leaves me with one huge question." Tony put both hands on the bar, peering over Bianca and Olivia's shoulders at everyone else in the room. "Who's Rick's next target? An APB ain't gonna stop him."

"Got to be one or more of you four." Lynn twirled her hair with one hand, pointing at Olivia, Tony, Bianca, and the space Horace probably occupied. "But only time will tell us who."

"It better be me." Tony cracked his knuckles. "If it's not, he's gonna wish it were 'cause I'm sick of waiting."

NIGHT CREW

A PROVIDENCE PARANORMAL COLLEGE
SHORT STORY

"Dammit, Professor," Lynn Frampton glared down at the patient in the ICU. "Why won't you wake up?"

"We still don't know," I said, "but you're on the list of people we'll call when he does."

"Me?" The girl turned and blinked. "That makes no sense."

"All the same, it was what he wanted. You're on his shortlist, Miss Frampton."

"But I haven't even known him for a year."

"There's another student with a similarly brief acquaintance listed." I crossed my arms.

"Let me guess, you're not going to tell me who else is on that list."

"You're as smart as he was at your age."

"Uh, what?" The mundane girl pulled one ear lobe. "I think I heard you say something about this old coot as though you knew him back when he was my age."

"I did." I grinned. "But visiting hours are over now. You'll be back again at the same time next week?"

"No, not then, or the one after, either." Lynn shouldered her bag. "There's this weird gap between summer sessions at the college and when fall semester starts. I have to go home for that."

"We'll see you in a few weeks, then." I stepped aside to let her past.

"Yeah." She paused in the doorway. "You think it makes a difference? Me coming in here and reading to him, I mean?"

"I'm sure it does." I listened to her sniffle, but gave no indication I'd heard it. "He came in here about a week before it happened, telling me he wanted your name at the top of the list when you get through Extrahuman med school, you know."

"No, I didn't know." Nut-brown hair flipped over Lynn's shoulder to hang down her back. "I never even mentioned my major to him."

"Well, he knew, and he thinks you have what it takes to study and work here."

"Wow."

"That's what I said when he told me you were a freshman."

"Well, I'd tell you to take good care of him, but that's already happening. So keep on keeping on."

"I will. It's what I do."

The girl left, taking her enormous brain with her. I wasn't all that certain she wasn't a little bit Psychic. Nate Watkins had never been one to wax sentimental about anyone or anything, practically since birth. I should know since I was there.

Working in the hospital legitimately was more than I'd ever dared dream of either before or during the Big Reveal. When Henry Baxter and his friends rescued me from the last Extramagus to plague Providence, I'd been working as one of two night doctors for the then-secret extrahuman community. I'd delivered babies for Psychics, Magi, shifters, and even vampires like me. I'd pulled enough iron, silver, and copper out of faeries and shifters to fill a dumpster, and I'd cured enough extrahumans of magical sicknesses and poisons to fill this hospital a hundred times over.

"Doctor Klein to the nurse's station."

I still got a chuckle at hearing my name over the intercom, so I sauntered down to see what the most important staff members on the ICU floor wanted from literally old me. But it wasn't the nurses who'd called for a moment of my time after all.

"Cal." I put my hands on my hips as I faced my ex-husband. "I thought I told you not to visit me here."

"It's police business this time, Agnes."

"Providence is hardly the jurisdiction of Newport PD." I kept my tone icy even though it'd do nothing to defend me against hospital gossip.

"All the same, I'm investigating something from Newport that ties back here."

"Couldn't you have sent it to Dennison?" I preferred dealing with the Alpha lady at the Providence PD since I'd gone legit and started working here.

"No," Cal replied. "It might have something to do with Stephanie."

I blinked, unable to speak. If he'd found any unexplored angles, I'd drop everything to hear him out. Stephanie was our daughter, and her disappearance was the reason we'd split. Even after all this time, news about her would stop me in my tracks. He knew it, too.

"Agnes?"

"Okay, Cal." I let my hands drop. "I'll help. Step into my office."

I had no such thing, so I led him into a utility room. I didn't want the nurses worrying their practical heads about my problems, and I also kept my personal affairs on a need-to-know basis. From what I understand, it is a fairly common thing for vampires turned before the Reveal to do.

"So, what's your case, and how does it relate to our daughter?" I stood between Cal and the door, doing my best to make him feel cornered. It worked.

"Um, well." Cal tugged his collar as though he was still a beat cop in a uniform, like he'd been when we first met. The gesture looked all wrong with his t-shirt. "We got some reports about a musician down in Newport for the big Battle of the Bands this summer. He's a vamp from the Jazz era. He helped us bust a blood-doll ring back during the Reveal."

"And this has to do with Stephanie, how?"

"The ring in question had operated since the sixties. This guy, Jack Steele, reconnected with another girl who was involved—a victim. Della Dawn. Maybe she saw Stephanie."

Our daughter had gone missing in 1983, almost seven years before the Reveal. One of the points of contention between Cal and me was his theory that blood traffickers got her. I couldn't stomach the idea, but he'd conducted his investigation based on it. As the decades wore on and my work went legitimate, my stance had softened. Statistics can lie but not that much.

"Maybe." I leaned against the door. "We both know Dampyr were in big demand back then."

"Probably still are." Cal sighed, running one hand through his hair. "Old habits die hard. Anyway, I also wanted some help with toxicology kits for vamps. Newport's extrahuman ward is under-funded, so there are none to spare. It'll help if I can test some crucial evidence in Della's case."

"Sure." I stepped past him, reaching for a box on the top shelf. "They're in here." I pulled a few out and handed them over."

"Thanks, Agnes."

"You know the chances of us finding anything about her are slim."

"I know."

"Calvin, she's probably dead." I looked him full in the face, a rush of emotion coming back to me like life to my limbs after feeding. Destiny sucked. My heart wanted him back but my head disagreed. Or maybe my pride.

"No, Agnes." My ex-husband stowed the kits in the inside pocket of the ridiculously puffy vest he wore, the one Stephanie had bought him because of that stupid movie about the time-traveling kid. His tenacious grip on foolish hopes was the reason I couldn't deal with his place in my heart anymore. "You're wrong."

"Your stupid hunches don't mean I'm wrong. You're not a Precog or a Scryer." Psychometry was Calvin's talent, one that only worked once he'd found physical evidence.

"But Steph was too special to pass through a morgue unnoticed."

"You know what, Cal? Do you know which of the patients in this damn hospital are special?"

I tapped my foot, waiting for an answer. Cal gave me nothing but a shrug.

"All of them are special! Every single person, human or extra, who rolls in here? They each matter. They're all someone's kid or parent or uncle or professor, and every single one of them is going to leave this world someday. Even ghosts move on, Cal."

"We don't."

"I know. And you know what? It sucks!"

"So why do—" Cal waved his hand at the shelves, the sink, the door. "All this? Why bother then, Agnes, if you've got no hope? If this is how you feel?"

"You keep your hope. Detectives need that. Doctors don't. All we need is a reason to fight. We do that for hopeless cases too, because everyone is special. As special as our completely mortal Dampyr daughter, no more, no less."

"Jeez, Agnes." Cal stretched one hand toward me. "I'm sorry."

"In all my centuries, I have never waited this long for an apology. But I'll accept it, Cal." I took his hand, squeezing. It felt freeing to touch another person whose skin was the same temperature as my own. "If you'll accept mine. I'm sorry, too."

"Thank you." Cal squeezed back. "But it won't stop me from investigating. No matter what I find, it'll be worth it to me. I hope you understand."

"I think maybe we understand each other better now than when we were married." I let my hand linger.

"What took you so long to tell me? Is this is the way you always thought about practicing medicine?"

"December is always slower than May, Cal." I gave him a grin. "It takes us longer than you younger vamps to get around to just about anything personal."

"I'll keep that in mind during my investigation." He let go of my hand.

"Good." I stepped aside, giving him a clear path to the door. "Keep it in mind afterward as well."

"Okay!" His smile lit the tiny room. "I'll come back with anything I find."

"Good." He held the door open for me. "Don't be a stranger."

I turned down the hall, looking back over my shoulder as he headed in the opposite direction, toward the elevator. I entertained the thought that maybe coincidence had known what it was doing, putting us together. Moments later, I let that wishful thought slip into the depths of my long memory. I let Calvin take all of my hope with him as he went. He needed it more than I did, after all.

SIGNS POINT TO YES
A PROVIDENCE PARANORMAL COLLEGE
SHORT STORY

Jan Washburn sat behind the reception desk at Shady Acres. A resident sailed past, literally. Mr. Meyer had the power of levitation. Jan got up, leaving her post even though she technically wasn't supposed to. There was no technicality about Mr. Meyer using his psychic abilities in the lobby or being off the dementia ward. She strode, stretching long legs now achy with her advancing age. Jan wasn't sure exactly when or how she'd developed the ground-eating pace, but it sure came in handy when residents played Houdini.

This wasn't the first time she'd had to follow a Houdini from Dementia. Mrs. Perri had Mind magic, which let her convince half-asleep night-shift aides to open the door for her. Jan knew Mr. Meyer had gone it alone, however. His Telekinesis worked on mundane locks. The director would have to invest in some magipsychic deterrents in the future.

"Wasn't it nice to see Lane the other night?" Jan smiled at Mr. Meyer even though she couldn't turn her head all the way in his direction without the risk of bumping a food or laundry cart.

"Lane?" The old psychic shook his head. "I already told the

wife she ain't naming the baby after that cockamamie movie character. Teased is all a handle like that'll get a kid."

"Oh." Jan knew she had to travel back in time with Mr. Meyer. Arguing with a man capable of bringing the entire building down on their heads was not an option.

"Anyway, I gotta get back. The nurse said it'll be any time now, and I want to be there when the little kicker comes out."

"Sure, I understand." Jan didn't. She'd never had a child. "Let me walk with you."

"Fine."

Mr. Meyer maintained his blistering pace past the dark and empty dining room, the locked garden gate, and through the open double doors to the rehab ward. Jan stayed close, unsure of what the poor man's reaction would be when he didn't find a maternity room with his wife inside. He stopped abruptly in front of an old framed photograph. Jan's sneakers squeaked on linoleum as she joined him.

"Huh." Mr. Meyer scratched his head. "I don't remember seeing that guy before."

"Guy?" Jan's fingertip pressed against her right temple and she blinked.

"Yeah." He jerked his chin at the upper left corner. "Guy in the Greek fisherman's cap."

The photo was from one of Jan's outings with the ladies from Shady Acres' long-term ambulatory unit. They'd gone on a Trolley Tour in Providence and taken the snapshot in front of the Biltmore Hotel. It'd been a ladies-only trip, so what was that round-faced and bearded man doing in the back of their trolley?

"I don't remember him either," said Jan. "And I was there."

"The mind plays more tricks than a Kitsune in a contest with a Tanuki." Mr. Meyer folded his arms over his chest. "I bet he was always in that snapshot, and that fact just fell out of our heads like a penny from a holey pocket."

"Really?"

"Yeah." Mr. Meyer shrugged. "I get the idea it's something I'm used to. You aren't."

"Aren't what, Mr. Meyer?"

"Used to the holes in your memory." He peered at Jan. "You make a good show of not having them, but I know it when I see it. Takes one to know one, if you get my drift."

"Um, no. I've got a perfectly normal memory." Jan didn't dare move, and could barely breathe. Mr. Meyer was right. Retrograde amnesia wasn't anything like normal. Jan wondered how one Telekinetic with Alzheimer's could have guessed her weakness when Precognitive and Telepathic Psychics with the same condition hadn't.

Enough of Jan was missing to justify a picture of her brain on the side of a milk carton. The absent years were the whole reason she'd taken a job here at Shady Acres. The folk on the Dementia ward lost more of themselves each day, but Jan's memory loss remained static, a zero-sum game.

Her denial came without full understanding of why she made it, a knee-jerk reaction so automatic she'd never thought to question it before. She glanced at Mr. Meyer, forgetting again that she hadn't remembered.

"No." He placed his hands on his hips, first the right, then the left. "Don't look at me. Look at the other guy who shouldn't be there."

Mr. Meyer's lucidity was still common enough to be a relief instead of a red flag. Psychics with dementia got possessed or influenced on occasion, and too much lucidity at the wrong time could mean something else had taken up residence. She'd have to tell the nurse on his ward about that, of course.

Jan turned her gaze back to that photo, meeting the eyes of the image of the man who shouldn't be there. Something glinted on his left hand—a wedding band. She'd seen that before, and the man, too. Her eyes locked on his face and it melted her heart.

"Edgar?" The name escaped her lips, leaving what felt like a chasm where her heart should be. Jan clenched her left hand, twisting it in the buttoned yoke on her standard-issue Shady Acres Staff polo shirt. "Is that my Edgar?"

"That's Edgar Watkins, brother of that professor down at the Paranormal College. Been missing for a pile of years." Mr. Meyer's brow wrinkled like slouching socks, the corners of his mouth tilted down as he grappled with his slippery recall. "Is he really yours?"

The photo, frame and all, sailed off the wall and hovered in front of Jan's face. She couldn't look away, but her right hand covered her left, feeling the empty space on her ring finger. Had she worn a ring like Edgar's? Yes, she had, but Jan had no idea how she'd gained or lost it.

"Reply hazy, try again." Jan studied the photograph's mystery man again. What little of his face was not covered by hat or beard was solitary, well-used, and careworn. Jan knew it had once been unlined and filled with hope, but her mind kept it dim and flickeringly lit by the tiniest flame of memory.

"I know those Watkins brothers." Mr. Meyer plucked the frame from where it hovered and turned it toward him. "Well, 'knew' is a better way to put it, I guess. They're both psychics like me. Like you, too, Joyce."

"My name's Jan." A sense of the world tilting made her brace her feet and set her jaw. The sensation always came before a bout of future sight. "And my precognition's been dormant for over five years."

"Nah. You think those things, but you're wrong."

"I'm not the one with a room on the other side of this building." Jan gripped her biceps and shuddered, teeth chattering enough to almost mask the tap of approaching footsteps.

"And that's why I can remember all this when you can't." Mr. Meyer chuckled. "They didn't bother wiping my mind, you see." He tapped his forehead. "No point, when my noggin's scrambled up with more protein than an Atkins Diet omelet. But I have my lucid moments."

"No way to tell if this is one of them, though, old man." A tattooed hand clapped Mr. Meyer on the shoulder. "Come on back with me, okay?"

"Not now, Lane." Mr. Meyer looked up at his son's face, unfazed by the green hair that framed it. "This is maybe the most important thing I still have left to do."

"What? The conversation with Jan?"

"Joyce, not Jan." Mr. Meyer gave one sharp nod. "She has to hear the truth. I think she's about to get the picture, that it's time for her to remember."

"But Dad!"

"It's okay, Lane." Jan hobbled over to the nearest bench, knees about to fold down and out from under her. "Let him stay for now. He's onto something."

"Damn skippy, I am." Mr. Meyer floated the picture over to Jan, tilting it as he did. It flipped from landscape to portrait until the group of smiling ladies and the shadowy man hiding in the trolley had turned on their heads.

Something between the photo backing and the rear panel of the frame rattled, then hissed as it slid over the felt and paper. The whole contraption bounced three times, Mr. Meyer's Telekinesis in as much control as hands.

Something shiny bounced out and landed in Jan's lap. It gleamed like a thin metallic snake with a silver hide and a round, golden head. She managed not to scream. Instead, she reached down and peered at it.

The "head" was a simple gold band of the wedding variety, strung on a silver chain. Battered and scratched, the soft metal told a story if its life before its picture-frame hideaway, a story Jan thought she should have known. She didn't.

"I have a feeling."

"Well, duh," said Lane. "You're surrounded by psychics."

"She is one, kid." Mr. Meyer sighed. "She just doesn't remember."

"And you do?" Lane scratched his head. "You sure, old man?"

"I'm lucid for now, and one of the things I know is that there ring's a memory charm. She'll remember what she is as sure as you do every night, Lane."

"What am I, then?" Lane put his hands on his hips. "You never remember when I come to visit."

"Vamp." Mr. Meyer hung his head. "Summoner, too, like that lady friend of yours who's been here with you the last few months."

"Geez, Dad." Lane closed his eyes. "Wow."

Mr. Meyer clapped his son on the shoulder. Lane reached back, and in a New York minute, they were a tangle of arms and tears.

Jan sat staring at the ring on the chain, wondering whether she should touch it. She looked at the vampire and then his father, the years a visible chasm between them, exactly as she knew the Alzheimer's divided them further and in a less obvious way. But not now. Tonight was more magical than balls with glass slippers or a sleeping curse lifted.

Tonight, Lane and his father truly recognized each other for the first time in years, a brief and shining moment more ephemeral than Camelot.

Would touching her skin to the ring break this spell of lucidity? Should Jan play Mordred and break the Meyers' fleeting ideal kingdom? Could she bring herself to turn their world upside-down in this rare moment, after it had managed to right itself for once?

"Do I have to?" Jan's voice escaped, squeaking and choked like a mouse in a trap.

"Yeah." Mr. Meyer gave his son one more pat on the back before pulling away. "You've got to. What you know might just save the world."

Jan looked at Lane.

"My old man's right." The green-haired vampire gazed at the scuffed doodles on the toes of his sneakers. "You listen to him. I always did."

Jan reached for the ring, laid her hand on top of it, and curled her fingers to scoop it up.

Unfastening the chain was easy. Jan tossed the silver strand at the wastebasket, then slipped that ring on the third finger of her left hand where it belonged.

Mr. Meyer's eyes went vacant, his brow a confused wrinkle. Lane's shoulders drooped. Their world had turned turtle again, and hers had finally righted itself after twenty years. She wasn't Jan Washburn.

Her real name was Joyce Watkins, and she recalled that man in the Greek fisherman's cap. She remembered everything.

GHOST OF A CHANCE

The series continues with *Ghost of a Chance,* coming soon to Amazon and Kindle Unlimited.

CONNECT WITH THE AUTHOR

Find D.R. Perry Online

Website: https://drperryauthor.com/

Author Central: http://www.amazon.com/-/e/B00O6851HO

Facebook: https://www.facebook.com/drpperry/

Mailing List: https://app.mailerlite.com/webforms/
landing/p9i8u6

Twitter: https://twitter.com/DRPerry22

ALSO BY D.R. PERRY

Providence Paranormal College

Bearly Awake (Book 1)

Fangs for the Memories (Book 2)

Of Wolf and Peace (Book 3)

Dragon My Heart Around (Book 4)

Djinn and Bear It (Book 5)

Roundtable Redcap (Book 6)

Better Off Undead (Book 7)

Ghost of a Chance (Book 8)

Nine Lives (Book 9)

Fan or Fan Knot (Book 10)

Hawthorn Academy

Familiar Strangers (Book 1)

Gallows Hill Academy

Year One: Sorrow and Joy (coming soon)

For other books by DR Perry please see her Amazon author page.

OTHER LMBPN PUBLISHING BOOKS

To be notified of new releases and special promotions from LMBPN publishing, please join our email list:

http://lmbpn.com/email/

For a complete list of books published by LMBPN please visit the following pages:

https://lmbpn.com/books-by-lmbpn-publishing/

CPSIA information can be obtained
at www.ICGtesting.com
Printed in the USA
BVHW031030290621
610724BV00009B/237